wanamurraganya
THE STORY OF JACK McPHEE

'I see it as the story of a working man, and I think working men who read it will understand because they know the struggle. Then I also see it as the story of Wanamurraganya, the son of a tribal Aborigine. Then again, it's the story of a man who is fighting with being black and white. A man who chooses not to live in the tribal way, but who can't live the whiteman's way because the Government won't let him. I could go on and on, because what I'm really saying is, it's the story of many people, and they're all me!'

'I'm roughly eight-four now and I've been through a lot in my life. I have to tell you that it's only as you get to the end of your life that you start to realise what things are really important to you. I've been through the Exemption Certificate and Citizenship and I've struggled to live up to the whiteman's standard, but here I am, old, and good for nothing, and what keeps coming back to me? Dances, singing, stories the old people used to tell. Every night I lie in bed and sing myself to sleep with all my old corroboree songs. I go over and over them and I remember that part of my life. They're the things I love, they're the things I miss.'

Jack McPhee

Sally Morgan was born in Perth, Western Australia, in 1951. She completed a Bachelor of Arts degree at The University of Western Australia in 1974. She also has post-graduate diplomas from The Western Australian Institute of Technology (now Curtin University of Technology) in Counselling Psychology and Computing and Library Studies. She is married with three children.

As well as writing, Sally Morgan has also established a national reputation as an artist. She has works in numerous private and public collections both in Australia and North America. *Wanamurraganya* is her second book. Her first book, *My Place*, became an instant national bestseller, and has been published to considerable acclaim in Britain and North America.

Photograph by Paul Morgan.

wanamurraganya
THE STORY OF JACK McPHEE

Jack McPhee, 1987.

wanamurraganya
THE STORY OF JACK McPHEE

Sally Morgan

FREMANTLE ARTS CENTRE PRESS

First published October 1989 by
FREMANTLE ARTS CENTRE PRESS
193 South Terrace (PO Box 320), South Fremantle
Western Australia, 6162.

Reprinted October 1989 twice.
Mass paperback edition October 1990.

Consultant Editor B.R. Coffey
Designed by John Douglass.
Production Manager Helen Idle.

Typeset in 11/12 pt Century Book by Caxtons, Perth, Western Australia, and printed on 80gsm Vagabond by The Book Printer, Maryborough, Victoria.

National Library of Australia
Cataloguing-in-publication data

Morgan, Sally, 1951 -
    Wanamurraganya.
    ISBN 0 949206 99 7.
    1. McPhee, Jack. [2]. Aborigines, Australia - Western
    Australia - Biography. I. Title.
994.1'0049915

For
the people of the Pilbara
and those who come after me

Jack McPhee

ACKNOWLEDGEMENTS

The preparation and writing of *Wanamurraganya* were partly funded by the Australian Bicentennial Authority as a contribution to the celebration of the Australian Bicentenary in 1988. Grateful acknowledgement is also due to Dr Alan Dench and Professor Bob Tonkinson of The University of Western Australia, John Priestly of the Western Australian Department for Community Services, and the staff of the J.S. Battye Library of West Australian History for their assistance in the preparation of this work.

Some of the personal names included in this book have been changed, or only first names given, to protect the privacy of those concerned.

The creative writing programme of Fremantle Arts Centre Press is assisted by the Australia Council, the Australian Federal Government's arts funding and advisory body.

Fremantle Arts Centre Press receives financial assistance from the Western Australian Department for the Arts.

CONTENTS

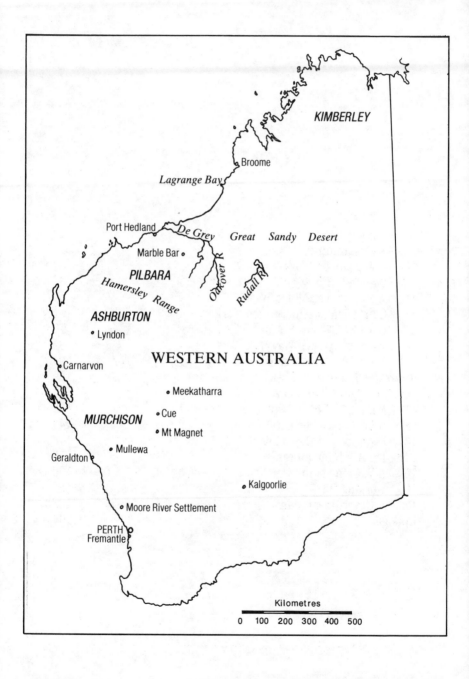

KIMBERLEY

Broome

Lagrange Bay

Port Hedland

De Grey

Great Sandy Desert

Marble Bar

Oakover R.

Rudall R.

PILBARA

Hamersley Range

ASHBURTON

Lyndon

Carnarvon

WESTERN AUSTRALIA

Meekatharra

Cue

MURCHISON

Mt Magnet

Mullewa

Geraldton

Kalgoorlie

Moore River Settlement

PERTH
Fremantle

Kilometres

0   100   200   300   400   500

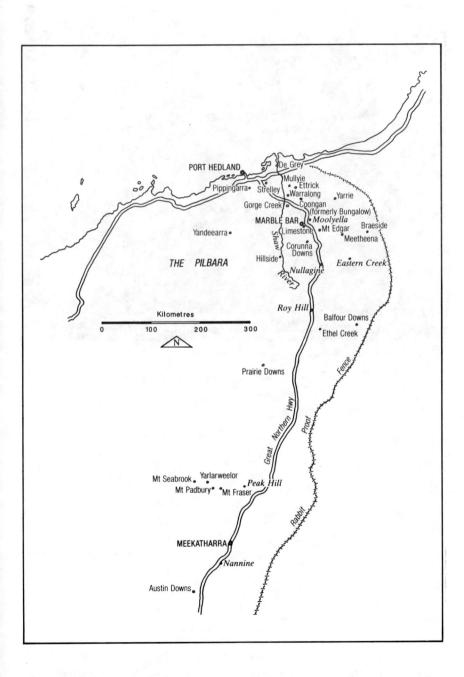

PORT HEDLAND

De Grey

Mullyie
Ettrick
Pippingarra
Warralong
Strelley
Yarrie
Gorge Creek
Coongan
(formerly Bungalow)

MARBLE BAR
Moolyella
Limestone
Mt Edgar
Braeside

Yandeearra
Meetheena

Corunna
Downs

Hillside
Nullagine
Eastern Creek

THE PILBARA

Shaw River

Roy Hill
Balfour Downs

Ethel Creek

Kilometres

0   100   200   300

N

Prairie Downs

Great Northern Hwy

Fence

Proof

Mt Seabrook
Yarlarweelor
Peak Hill
Mt Padbury
Mt Fraser

Rabbit

MEEKATHARRA

Nannine

Austin Downs

Jack McPhee and Sally Morgan, Port Hedland, 1985.

INTRODUCTION

I met Jack in May 1983 when I was researching my first book, *My Place*. I had gone to Port Hedland not knowing anyone but hoping to make contact with older people from the Port Hedland/Marble Bar area who remembered my grandmother and her brother. My grandmother had originally come from Corunna Downs Station, near Marble Bar. She was taken away as a child and brought down to Perth, as were other members of her family, in the days when black women weren't allowed to raise children fathered by whitemen. We had been given Jack's name and address by a friend of a friend who was working in Hedland at the time.

We felt very nervous just turning up and asking questions, but there was no other way for us to go. Fortunately, when we arrived at Jack's house he was sitting outside in the shade. He must have wondered who the vanload of strangers were. There was my husband Paul and I, three children and my mother, Gladys. Jack proved to be very friendly and we were immediately impressed by his strong character and sense of humour. He was the first person we approached and the first to tell us he knew exactly who we were talking about. In that moment, he became very special, because he confirmed the reality of our search for our extended family. The way he talked of my grandmother's sister brought home the fact that it was all real. These people had existed and were known, and through hearing people like Jack talk, we could know them too.

After we returned to Perth from the North I began writing to

Jack. A friendship developed from that correspondence and he decided he would like to spend Christmas with us. It was 1983, and this first stay proved to be a turning point. Jack was very interested in my writing and told me he had done some recording with various people over the years but that it had never amounted to anything. He wanted to know my reasons for writing and how I went about it. We had many talks where we discussed why it is important to record the lives of older people. Jack had a natural sense of history, he believed we should know the past and learn from it. He also felt it was important to communicate to young people what their older relations had been through. Once we decided to write the book there was no turning back.

Writing someone's life story is not a simple task. There are always expectations and reservations on both sides. For me, writing Jack's story meant doing his washing, ironing, cooking, taking him to the bank, post office and on social outings, arranging for him to catch up with people from his past, and of course introducing him to the delights of the Burswood Casino, for which I thank Paul and my mother.

For Jack, sharing his life meant putting up with hundreds of questions, going over the same incidents and experiences time and time again, discussing difficult areas that he had never talked about before, putting up with three cats (he hates them!), three noisy children and my cooking.

The point I'm trying to make is that the writing came as a natural outcome of the relationship that was unfolding between us rather than being the result of a more academic exercise. I recall when we were out once and Jack told someone I was writing his story. I quipped, 'Yes, I know more about him than he knows about himself!' Jack thought this was really funny, he said. 'You know that's true, now when I forget half a story I get you to finish it off because you know it so well!'

The first rule with this kind of writing is to begin where the teller wants to. We began by recording the names of every Afghan camel driver in the North-West that Jack could remember. Then we went on to railway sidings and windmills. It was only after that that Jack decided he would like to talk about his childhood. Most other people are reasonably comfortable with childhood because they are distanced from it and to some extent have come to terms with it. There will still be sensitive areas and this requires patience on behalf of the recorder. At first I never interrupted Jack with any questions because he was still becoming comfortable with the process. Instead I would make the occasional note, knowing that I could come back and ask him later when he was more relaxed. Jack took to staying with us for three months at a time. After his first stay we had recorded thirty one-hour tapes. When he returned home I set about transcribing them. In our times apart we would ring each other.

From these tapes I had a very rough outline of his life. Jack was particularly good at recalling dates, so from photocopies of my transcriptions I was able to cut and paste all the information he had given me into a rough chronological order. This process itself led to another set of questions. When I next saw Jack I showed him what I had done and proceeded with my questions. It became a format which we now fell into easily and happily. The answers to these questions were then transcribed and fitted into the first text. This meant that the text was changing, growing and being corrected and re-written continually.

Retelling is vital because often new details or perspectives are added which give greater depth to what at first might have seemed a fairly superficial story. Also, people store memories differently. What might appear to be a simple question requiring a one sentence answer might only be able to be answered fully and accurately by the teller within the broader context of a much more involved story.

The teller has to be kept fully informed and aware of what is being written and how the book is proceeding. There may be things which the writer might like to include but which the teller objects to. In this case the final decision always belongs to the teller. Also, sometimes the interests of the community, especially specific Aboriginal communities, must be weighed against the right of an individual to impart certain information. When trying to make the book flow the writer will have to add joining sentences and words so the book is readable, this has to be done in an unobtrusive way and in a manner that the teller is happy with.

Over a period of three years, Jack and I went through this process six times. It was very laborious but absolutely necessary. In the later stages I would get Paul to ask him questions. Jack and he were great friends by then and he enjoyed having a man to converse with for a change.

Once the book was getting towards the final stage I worked in the J.S. Battye Library of West Australian History, checking spellings, dates, people, stations and photographs. At the same time Jack and I were able to get his personal file from the Department of Community Services. This consisted of some three hundred pages and, while it told me nothing new, it was very useful in confirming dates, movements and the general attitudes of the times. Jack of course took a great interest in all these things that had been written about him by people who were then in authority. I read the whole file to him and we had a good laugh. There was one particular incident which I found interesting. A report by the Protector of Aborigines asserting that he had spoken to Jack about his forthcoming marriage at Moore River Settlement. Jack laughed when I read it to him. It seems that the Protector had interviewed Arthur Neal, the white superintendent of the settlement, who had told him how Jack felt. This was then reported officially as being an interview with Jack. There are times when an oral account is far more reliable than a written one.

Of course there are constraints in this kind of work as in any other. There was the obvious one of Jack being a male who had been through the Law and me being not only female but related as well. Also, I had to accept that there would be certain information shared which he did not want me to include in the book.

When the book was in final draft, Paul read it to him in its entirety. Jack's hearing had become progressively worse and it was now easier for him to listen to Paul's voice than mine. This reading is very important. The teller has to know his confidences have been kept, his stories have not been distorted, and his life has been communicated in a manner in which he himself would speak.

Our final decision was regarding the cover. Originally, it was going to be an old photo, but the quality was poor, so we decided I should do a painting. One night I asked Jack to describe Wanamurraganya and as he talked I drew.

'Does this drawing have the feel of that place?', I asked him.

16

'Nearly. Flatten out those hills a bit, and you need some reeds near the water.'

When I showed him my next attempt he said, 'No, no, that's no good, the hills are still too bumpy. Here, give me the pencil.'

I watched as he slowly changed my drawing. Finally he said, 'Ah, that's it. You can paint that now.' And so the cover was born.

In creating this book, our common purpose was to communicate to others a feeling of what it was like for someone like Jack to live during a certain period of our history.

Just before he went back North after his story was finished, I asked him how he felt about it. His reply sums up what the book is about.

'I see it as the story of a working man, and I think working men who read it will understand because they know the struggle. Then I also see it as the story of Wanamurraganya, the son of a tribal Aborigine. Then again, it's the story of a man who is fighting with being black and white. A man who chooses not to live in the tribal way, but who can't live the whiteman's way because the Government won't let him. I could go on and on, because what I'm really saying is, it's the story of many people, and they're all me!'

Sally Morgan

1

My Beginnings
1905-1912/13

I think I was born around 1905, it could have been earlier. Some say I'm older, but nobody really knows. We didn't have birth certificates in those days. I date myself roughly by what others say and my earliest memories. These things never used to be important but you need dates now for Government papers and things like that. Also, I'm proud of my memory. I reckon it's pretty good to be my age and remember what I do.

My mother was a ngayarda banujutha*, tribal Aborigine. Her black name was Marduwanyjawurru, her white name was Mary. She had four sisters: Mugaari or Eva, Nyamalangu (Nellie), Ngarlgaari (Fanny) and Yarriwawurru (Dinah). Her people spoke Light Naml and belonged to the area of land where the Oakover and Davis Rivers cross, about one hundred and ten miles out of Marble Bar. It's not bad country there, many rivers criss-cross that area so there's always water to keep you going. Her people had lived there from generation to generation.

My family name is Yirrabinya, roughly translated it means teeth. It could have had another more significant meaning many years ago, but I have no knowledge of it. There are four skin groups where I come from: Banaga, Burungu, Milangga and Garimarra. My skin group is Garimarra. This is very important because it determines my relationship to everyone else in the area. On the basis of my skin I will relate to others as my mother, father, uncle,

---

* Ngayarda banujutha: a person whose ancestry is entirely Aboriginal.

son and so on. It means that even when I lose relatives close to me I always have a mother, father, uncle in the skin way.

My mother only had two children that lived, me and my brother Walyayingu (Jim Watson). He was a ngayarda banujutha and ten years older than me. I think my mother had me late in life because I remember her being older than the other women with young children. Also, she knew many old corroboree songs, not everyone could sing the ones she could. In those days the people loved singing, everyone sang, it wasn't just the job of a few. When I was very small I remember sitting and watching my mother and aunties all dancing in a line. They looked so pretty with their painted body markings and cockatoo feathers. It was wonderful.

My Aboriginal father came from the same area as my mother. His real name was Ngawarrangu, but whites called him Bandy Jim. He died before my mother and was buried near a spring on Mt Edgar Creek which runs through Mt Edgar Station. There are a lot of springs in that area. The Aboriginal name for the spring where he was buried is Wanamurraganya. This name is also given to the bulbs that grow there. You can pull them up, dry them out and then grind them up to use for damper. They are Wanamurraganya, the food, that comes from Wanamurraganya, the water.

My people call me Wanamurraganya because of the old man. Sometimes they will say, Wanamurraganyaurru. Wanamurraganya is my name and when you add 'urru' on, it means that I'm called that because it's the place where my father or some other relative is buried.

You see, my stepfather was an important man, very strong in the Law and highly respected. I was supposed to inherit his powers and follow after him, but things never worked out like that. Often when one of my friends sees me in the street he calls out, 'Hey Wanamurraganya!' That name has a lot of significance for the old days and the old people and I always answer to it.

The actual Aboriginal name my mother gave me was Juliingu, but no one ever calls me that. My white name is Jack, but my mother called me Jacky. I think she thought it was good for me to have a white name. People around the area came to know me as Jack.

19

When I was young I used to think that Sandy McPhee was the whiteman who sired me. His real name was Alec, Sandy was his nickname. He was a prospector brother to William McPhee who managed De Grey Station. Sandy was very kind to Mum and me. It wasn't until years later that I found out the truth; that he wasn't really my father.

Now, my Aboriginal father, Ngawarrangu, was quite notorious. It was he who killed Dr Ed Vines on Braeside Station around 1899. What happened was this. He was working on Braeside with my mother and her sister, Eva. The station owner, Hodgson, was cruel. According to old Jack Mitchell, who was a child on Braeside at the time, a woman and her unborn child had died because of a whipping he had given them. I don't know if that's true or not, but that's what they say.

It was Ngawarrangu's job to shepherd the sheep. There were quite a few of them and with no fenced paddocks it made it a difficult job. If he lost any sheep Hodgson gave him a hiding. He got very sick of this so he asked if my mother could go out and help him, but he got a boot in the guts for asking. Hodgson was mean with the tucker as well. If there was any bread, it was sour, he fed the people anything that was crook.

Ngawarrangu got fed up with this kind of treatment so he left and went over to the Balfour Downs area where he rounded up a wirri, that's an Aboriginal army. Now, you have to understand that it wouldn't have been possible for just any blackfella to do this. He could only do it because he was a maban man. The word maban means secret things to do with the spirit world, that's about the closest I can get to it in English.

A maban man has spiritual power. He can make things move without touching them. He can make devil-devil sticks take off like an aeroplane. He can kill someone and leave no mark. He has authority over people and spirits.

If a maban man wants to kill someone he has to stay away from whiteman's tucker because that will weaken his spirit. He's got to eat the food he was born for. The natural food, like goanna, emu and kangaroo. The food he was brought up on as a piccaninny. It's that food that will make him strong.

When he's built his strength up he can make his spirit leave his body and enter his enemy's body. While he's in there he sings that man and then when he leaves and returns to his own body he knows the man he has sung will soon sicken and die.

I'm telling you all of this to give to you an idea of the kind of man Ngawarrangu was. He wasn't just any maban man, he was an exceptionally powerful one.

Anyway, he rounded up about fifty men and they came to Braeside late at night and hid down near the river, which was about three-quarters of a mile from the homestead. At piccaninny daylight they crept in. There was a cattle dog tied up out the front. They hit him on the head so he wouldn't raise the alarm. Then Ngawarrangu slipped silently into the house and slowly climbed the stairs.

Unfortunately, the first whiteman to appear was Dr Vines. Ngawarrangu was in such a rush for revenge that he speared and killed Dr Vines before he realised it was the wrong man. There was a pregnant woman on the station at that time too, that's why Dr Vines was there, and the story goes that later my mother and her sister helped deliver the baby.

Ngawarrangu and the other men in the wirri left after that and soon the police were after them. Other Aborigines warned Ngawarrangu that the police would harm him if they caught him, so he started going by a different name. They arrested a couple of men found in the area and hanged them for the killing.

In the end they caught my stepfather too and put him in Roebourne gaol. It was a hanging gaol in those days so I don't think he wanted to stay too long.

One morning, when the warder brought him in his tucker, he was gone. No broken lock, no broken nails, the door shut tight, the window in place, nothing different. The police couldn't understand how he escaped, but my people could. He was a maban man, it was the magic way.

The police tracked him to the Hamersley Ranges and then gave up. Ngawarrangu worked his way round to Marble Bar where he picked up a sack of flour, which was a main food in those days. He kept out of sight and headed to what we call the Black Range, he was looking for my mother. Around sundown he caught up with her people, but when he saw that she was with another man he

Government Offices, Marble Bar, 1906. (Battye 23527P)

became very angry and picked up a barbed spear and speared his rival through the leg. Then he speared my mother in her leg but it wasn't as bad a wound and only went in a little bit. After that they were back together again.

Of course the story I've just told you happened long before I was born, but I know it well because it belongs to my family and has been passed down.

When I was a baby we spent quite a lot of time on Mt Edgar Station. Mum used to help with shepherding and milking the cows and Ngawarrangu used to tidy the yard. I made good friends with the Corboys' little daughter, Alma. The Corboys owned Mt Edgar.

One of my earliest memories is of Alma and me mucking around teasing a calf silly. When the mother cow saw what we were doing she got real cross and charged us. We ran for a big granite rock but couldn't get up because it was too slippery, so we just ran around and around it screaming for help. My mother finally heard us, she called out to us not to worry and came and herded the cow away. Then she growled at us for what we'd done, but she must have thought it was funny because she was laughing too.

That's one of the few memories I have of Mum. That, and the sound of her voice singing and talking to me.

We eventually left Mt Edgar and went to the Moolyella area because it was corroboree time. Ngawarrangu and Mum loved the singing and dancing, it was an important part of their lives.

There was a favorite dance that Ngawarrangu looked forward to. The singing for that dance told about a man raising his arm to the sky, holding a spear. He could be hunting an enemy or a kangaroo, but I think Ngawarrangu liked the idea of an enemy. The man who is hunting digs the point of the spear into his enemy's chest, oomph!, and then pulls it out again. You know I can still see him up there with his arm raised and then, oomph!, digging in the spear and oomph!, pulling it out again. Aah, Ngawarrangu really loved that one!

After the corroboree my mother got some work in Bert Watson's store, which was in the Moolyella tinfield area. Half of it was a pub and half a store and it sold whatever you needed; especially tinned food. I remember there was a cake in a tin then called Canterbury cake. It was lovely. They sold boiled lollies, flour, all sorts of odds and ends. There was another store a few miles away as well, run by a bloke whose first name was McDonald. The only other buildings around there were bush humpies which were made by the tin fossickers. It's always been an area rich in tin.

Even Marble Bar wasn't much to speak of in those days. The police station was the main building and it was made from stone and clay, not much cement around then, not like today. There wasn't a decent church built there until the 1940s.

My brother, Jimmy, was taking more of an interest in me then because I was a little bit older. When my mother was working he used to look after me. He would put me on a horse in front of him and take me down to visit the old people at their camp. They used to make a great fuss of me. I really looked up to my big brother Jimmy.

I have one memory, it's like a dream really. I was standing near Bert Watson's store and Jimmy must have done something wrong, because Bert punched him and then kicked him along the ground. Jimmy must have been fourteen or fifteen. I felt very upset that he was getting hurt and I took a strong dislike to Bert Watson

Ironclad Hotel, Marble Bar, c.1910. (Battye 5452P)

because of it.

Not long after that we left there and went to live with the old people. They spent their time panning for tin and then swapping it for food. We hadn't been with the old people long when my mother took sick and died. I can't recall her dying but I do remember the old ones making a fuss of me and not telling me. I never found out Mum had gone until a week later. Jimmy couldn't tell me because he was off working on a station at the time. I started looking for my mother and calling for her, so my aunties finally took me and showed me the grave. I guess I would have been about five years old then.

My Aunty Eva took me in as my Aunty Yarriwawurru (Dinah) went into Marble Bar to work at the police station doing cleaning and washing. She took her son Gubiingu (Jack Doherty) with her, he was two years younger than me and had been born with such bad eyesight that he was practically blind. I think that it must

24

have run in the family because I was born with only one good eye myself. I really missed Jack, he was one of my playmates. He had a brother called Jiliyangu (Clancy) who had been sent down to the Swan Native and Half Caste Mission the same time Albert and Arthur Brockman* went. Albert and Arthur were from Corunna Downs Station which was owned by the Drake-Brockmans then. One of my aunties was married to a Corunna Downs man and had lived there for many years. Albert and Arthur were related to me, I'm younger than them though. Lots of kids were taken away then, they were two that got caught up in it. Albert managed to return to his homeland but Arthur never did. Jack and Clancy's father was Mick Doherty, who owned Meetheena Station in partnership with Morris McKenna. I didn't get to meet Clancy until around 1923, we became very good friends later in life.

One of the people who was good to me then was my Uncle Hector, he was a big, solid man from the desert area. He used to sit me on his knee and sing corroborees. He was famous amongst the people as a songmaker. He sang in Balgoo and some of his corroborees would last over a week with many different parts to them.

Whenever Hector came up with a new song everyone was always amazed. They were all so different you see, so clever and so meaningful. There was a lot of respect for him because of this. When it came to song-making Hector was considered very special. How the whole thing worked out was like this. Hector would make all the different songs that were to be sung, then it was up to others to try and make a dance that would do credit to that song. This wasn't always easy because Hector's songs were so good people worried about having a dance that was up to standard. Hector had complete power to say yes or no to the dances that were invented. If he didn't like the dance or thought it wasn't good enough, it wasn't allowed to be performed. It was only when all this was settled that the corroboree went ahead. His songs became so famous that some even travelled up to the Kimberley area, as well as down to Meekatharra.

Even without my mother I was very happy there with the old

---

*   Albert and Arthur Brockman: Sally Morgan's maternal grandmother's brothers.

people, they were all related to me in one way or another and took good care of me. The trouble was, I was the sort of kid that loved to tease and this ended up causing me some bother and turning my life in another direction.

I was playing with some other kids in a pit one day when an old kangaroo dog called Mounter came over to us. If you've ever seen a roo dog you know they're big and fierce and you don't mess with them. So what did I do? Did I have any sense? No! I went straight up to him and teased him with a stick. He got sick of me and bit me on the head. Luckily, one of my uncles, Gudanyawurru, was close by and he speared Mounter through before he could bite me some more.

It was a bad bite and the people were worried about me getting sick so they sent word that help was needed. Frank Williams, the postmaster, and Corporal Strapp came out to pick me up in a buggy and pair from Marble Bar. Corporal Strapp would have had to come because in those days the police were also the appointed protectors of Aborigines and it was they who generally took the mardamarda* children away to missions and so on. They lifted me onto the buggy and took me to Marble Bar. I was feeling a little bit crook by then. My Aunty Eva came in too so I wasn't alone.

I was taken to see Dr Triado, who was very nice. He said, 'Now Jacky, you sit down there and eat this apple and while you're doing that I'll stitch up your head'. I suppose the apple was my dope!

When he finished he said, 'While you're here, you have to come and see me every morning Jacky so I can check your head and make sure it's mending properly'.

I was taken to live with Corporal Strapp then because my Aunty Dinah was still working there. The Strapps had a couple of boys and my cousin Jack Doherty was there so I felt quite happy about it. My aunty made a big fuss of me. When it came to kids, she was tender-hearted.

Jimmy dropped in to see me whenever he could and had a bit of a play and took me for rides. It was a pity that he was so much older than me because it meant our lives would go in

* Mardamarda: person of mixed Aboriginal-European ancestry.

26

Camel Team, Marble Bar, c. 1910. (Battye 5453P)

different directions and though we were important to one another we never shared the closeness that you can have when only a few years separate you.

The other visitor I had was Sandy McPhee. Ever since Mum had died he'd always come and seen me whenever he could and given me a bag of boiled sweets. He was very kind to me.

Corporal and Mrs Strapp were both lovely people, I can't complain about them at all. They treated Jack and I the same as their own boys and were good to us in every way. Corporal Strapp was very good natured. I'm sure he used to get sick of us following him around everywhere and going into his office and so on, but he never growled at us.

Mrs Strapp didn't like Jack and I walking around with nothing on, so she took to making clothes for us. She wanted us to look the same as her boys. She'd dress us up in the morning and send us off to play but we found the clothes were too stuffy so we'd take them off and come home naked. She got very sick of us doing this so in the end she tried to trick us by making clothes that buttoned down the back.

I remember the morning she put us in those clothes, she was

smiling and telling us how nice we looked, I think she thought she'd finally beaten us, and we were thinking she had too. However, when we were out playing and getting hot and stuffy again we realised that if we stood in front of one another we could quite easily unbutton each other's clothes. That's exactly what we did and when we came home naked at lunchtime Mrs Strapp just threw her hands in the air and gave up!

Jack and I were always getting up to tricks, I suppose all kids are a bit like that. I remember there was an old blackfella in one of the cells when we were there. We had to take him his food. He had a big, heavy ball tied to his leg so it was hard for him to move around, we used to roll it along so he could come out of his cell and sit and have his lunch under a tree. Of course we were never satisfied when it came to food. We'd get stuck into his beans at the same time that he was trying to eat them. Then when they were all gone we'd run back to Mrs Strapp and say, 'That old fella really hungry, he got to have more!' She always gave us another helping.

I remember Halley's Comet going over when I was in Marble Bar. There were some old people camped just out of Marble Bar town near Cemetery Creek and Jack and I were camped down near them. We were playing and playing and getting more and more tired. Finally, we laid down on the ground and went to sleep. It seemed like we'd only been asleep a few minutes when it was daylight again.

'Wake up', Jack said as he shook me. 'Must be morning, it's not so dark anymore'. I didn't want to wake up, I felt like I'd only just gone to sleep.

We looked up and saw this bright, pretty thing in the sky. We were too frightened to look at it for too long because we thought it might be devil-devil. We made each other scared about it and ran all the way home to the police station.

Every Sunday Jack and I would walk down to the old people's camp and visit them. We loved being with the old ones because they made a fuss of us and told us stories. This time when we went down they were having a little corroboree amongst themselves, singing and laughing. Suddenly, three policemen swooped down, I can't recall if Corporal Strapp was there or not, but there were

View of Marble Bar, 1916. (Battye 68899P)

a number of policemen stationed in the Bar then. It was a dog shooting expedition. The rule then was, one man one dog, but the old people just love dogs so much that they always seemed to end up with more than their quota. I think the policemen must have noticed this and decided it was time some were bumped off.

They were all wailing and crying as the dogs were being shot. Old Rosie hid her Fox Terrier under her dress. Jack and I were scared so we took off and headed for the Afghans' camp, which wasn't far away. They must have wondered what was going on because we ran in all out of breath shouting, 'Policeman shooting, policeman shooting!'

They grabbed us and hid us in their tents and said, 'You kids stay in there and don't come out till we tell you!'

Jack and I were whispering to one another in language, 'Ooh, policeman shoot dogs, he might shoot us too!' We were getting ourselves really worked up for nothing. It was the dogs they were after, not two silly kids.

I had been with Corporal Strapp six months when one day my aunty told me that he was going to take me to live with the Stuart brothers for a while as they needed a boy to help them with the cows. She said she would still see me every day, as they weren't far out of town, so I should go quietly with Corporal Strapp.

I did as Aunty said. You see, what I didn't know then was that because I was mardamarda I could be sent anywhere by the police, even to a mission far away or a government settlement. I think Aunty knew this and was hoping to avoid it. Even though she would rather have me with her, at least Stuarts' was close by.

The Stuart brothers had a dairy and vegetable garden at the back of the Coongan River. I was around six by then and used to help Black Billy Marr bring the cows in. When Stuarts delivered the milk round town in the sulky I had to hang on to the ladle and pass it over when it was needed. They treated me kindly when I was there but I think I was just too young to be of much use to them. After three months they took me in and gave me back to Corporal Strapp. Aunty was very pleased about that, I think she was hoping I might be allowed to stay permanently with her. She liked having me and Jack together because she'd lost Clancy to the Aborigines Department and it was like she had two sons again. Sometimes I used to ask her about my cousin Clancy but she'd just shake her head and say, 'Mission got 'im'. I think she preferred not to talk about it.

There was a very bad blow not long after I was returned to the police station. You had no warnings of cyclones in those days. You just had to take them as they came. The ship called the *Koombana* went down and somehow this really caught the imagination of the old Mulba* women. They thought of the *Koombana* as a mother ship bringing food and people across the seawater to land. They cried for that ship and the people who were lost and made a song about it.

---

* Mulba: the name by which Aboriginal people of the Port Hedland/Marble Bar area of Western Australia refer to themselves. It is believed that the name orginally applied only to people from more southerly regions but its adoption is now widespread throughout areas of the Pilbara, Ashburton and Murchison.

2

Going Out To Work
1912/13 -1918

Aunty came to me that same year and told me that I was going to be given to Tom Heddrich for a while. He lived in the Bar and had four cows that needed looking after. She told me not to worry as I could come and have all my meals with her and Jack so I would still be seeing them every day. I thought that was all right, so Corporal Strapp took me over to Tom and I slept there after that and did a little bit with the cows whenever he asked me.

However, what I didn't know was that Tom had bought a share in Gorge Creek Station with George Arthur. Gorge Creek was situated on the railway line about halfway between Port Hedland and Marble Bar. Tom wanted to take three hundred head of cattle out there and he decided I would go with him.

I didn't want to go. I was only a seven-year-old kid, not a man, I wanted to stay near my family. I asked Aunty and she told me I didn't have any choice. She explained that if it were up to her she would keep me for good but that Corporal Strapp had given me to Tom Heddrich and he owned me now so I had to do what I was told.

The day we left, Aunty was very broken up. She cried and cried. I think she was wondering if she would see me again and she didn't like the idea of me being with men, and no mother to look after me.

We were on the road for three days, and I was given the job of washing the dishes and bringing in the wood for the fire. I felt very lonely when we finally got to Gorge Creek Station, I thought there might be other kids waiting there, but there were none, only

Train on the Marble Bar to Port Hedland line, 1911. (Battye BA 548/28)

me. There were no women there either, I thought there might be some old Mulba there who might take a liking to me, but there was no one. None of the men there were interested in having a game with a kid, they were only interested in the cattle and the work and George Arthur turned out to be a bit rough. I wasn't used to that.

I don't know why they took me with them because I couldn't do much. I used to play around on my own and do the jobs they gave me. There were plenty of snakes on Gorge Creek, poisonous ones, so you had to be careful, we were killing them every day. The only good thing that I can remember of my first stay there was when a cattle buyer called Billy Hill came out in his T Model Ford. It was the first car I had ever seen. He gave us all a ride in it and I decided that one day I would save up and buy myself a motorcar, then I could go and visit aunty whenever I liked.

I had been with Tom on Gorge Creek for a few weeks when he decided to take me into Port Hedland with him. He had taken over the licence of the Esplanade Hotel and wanted to go in there and spend some time building his new business up. I was happy to be leaving the station but worried that I was getting further and further away from my aunty.

In Hedland I slept in the hotel the same as Tom and his daughters. There was a governess who looked after all of us kids. The only difference was that the girls were being taught how to read and write and I wasn't. I used to watch them sometimes and wonder what they were doing. I was interested in learning myself but was never given the opportunity. Tom told me that while I was living in the hotel I was to stay away from all the Aboriginal people and just stick to his family.

I was only there a few months when I was sent back to Gorge Creek. When I arrived someone told me that my brother, Jimmy, had just been through the Law and was a man now. I didn't really understand what that meant but it seemed like something important. It made me homesick though, just to hear someone mention a family name. I started to think about my aunties and Jack and felt very unhappy.

As I said before, George Arthur was rough with me. If I did anything even slightly wrong he gave me a hiding. Often it wasn't a deliberate mistake, it was just that I was young and didn't know any better, but I still got a hiding for it.

My only friends then were the sheep and cattle, I used to muck around with them. I was out of my teasing habit by then so they used to put up with me. When I got really low I would run away. It never did me any good because George would notice I was missing and come and get me. I was all the time trying to get back to my aunty and the old people. I missed them all the time and when I was on my own they were all I could think about.

There was only one occasion when I made a reasonably successful escape bid. George had to go away boring for water on another station so he got a new bloke in to mind Gorge Creek while he was gone. I just couldn't get on with the new manager. He never hit me or anything, but he growled at me all day. He didn't like kids and he went on and on. I couldn't do anything to please him.

I sneaked away at the break of dawn. I figured if this bloke disliked kids that much there was little chance that he would come after me. I followed the railway line for twenty-four miles and ended up near the Coongan Pub, which is another twenty-four miles from the Bar by road but a bit further by rail. It was run by Harry

Bell then. The first Coongan Pub had been owned by 'Cockrag' Robinson and had been built down near the river, but when the railway line went through, the pub was moved closer to the line. Coongan was a siding but not a settlement. Its main purpose was to service people that used to come in from the surrounding stations like Eginbah and Warralong.

My aim at this time was to get to the Bar to see my family but it was getting too dark to keep going so I hid down by the well. I was scared of sleeping in the bush on my own, so I thought if I waited until it got really dark, I could sneak closer to the pub and sleep there. I knew I would feel safer being near a building with people inside.

Suddenly, before I had a chance to move, a man appeared and spotted me. He called out to me and I froze. I thought if I ran he would only catch me so I just sat there. His name was Colin Campbell and he'd come down to get water for his horses.

'Where are you headed young fella?', he asked.

'Marble Bar.'

'And what do you want to go there for?'

'See my family.'

'Where have you come from?'

'Gorge Creek.'

'So you belong to George Arthur then.'

'Yeah.'

'You've walked a long way son. I don't think you should go on to the Bar, it'll only get you in trouble. How about if you stay with me? I've got horse drays and I cut wood for the puffing billy. You can give me a hand and I'll look after you all right. You won't want to run away.'

I really wanted to go to the Bar, but I felt I had to stay with this man because if I didn't he would probably report me to the police and then I would be sent back.

I stayed with Colin for three weeks and he was very good to me. I didn't mind working for him. He took me right into the pub with him and bought my meals, he was a nice fella.

George Arthur turned up for me after that and I was sorry to leave. I wanted to stay with Colin. I remember hearing them talk.

'Jacky's a good boy', Colin said, 'a real good boy, George. He's been a big help to me and he does what he's told.'

'Yes', said George, 'but he belongs to me, thanks for minding him though.'

I went back to Gorge Creek after that. I hadn't seen my family, but at least I'd had some nice company for a while.

Things improved a little after that because George had to travel back and forth around Warralong and Bungalow Stations doing odd jobs and he chose to take me with him rather than leaving me on the station. This meant that I got to meet some of my other relatives and mix with a few more kids.

I met up with my cousin Clancy McKenna during this time. His mother was my mother's sister Nellie, and his father was Morris McKenna, part owner, with Mick Doherty, of Meetheena Station. Aunty was very good to me. Clancy and I got on well together and it stopped me from missing Jack so much.

One day, when we were back on Gorge Creek, who should turn up but Sandy McPhee. He'd joined up and was off to fight Kaiser Bill in the war. He was very pleased to see me and asked George if he could take me into Hedland so I could see him off on the boat. I was really excited when George agreed.

Sandy gave me a real good time in Hedland. He bought me some new clothes and lots of lollies and whatever food I liked. The few days we spent together were wonderful. Before he left he gave me a few quid and told me to spend it on myself and that when he came back from the war he would come and see me again. I was very sad to see him go. Years later I learnt that Sandy had been killed at Gallipoli.

Tom Heddrich arranged for me to go back to Gorge Creek and I stayed there for a few more years.

Around 1918, when I was about thirteen, George Arthur took me with him to Warralong Station to sink a bore. While he was working I could see the shiny tin roof of the homestead glinting in the distance and all I could think of was that I had friends and relatives over there and would love to go and see them. I took off, it was only a few miles.

It was wonderful to see my friends again. They gave me something to eat and warned me not to be seen too soon or I might have to go back to George straight away. I stayed out of sight for a few days, but then I got gamer and started hanging around the homestead, getting my food and playing with the other kids.

Then I got really confident and started going down to the yards to watch a big bloke called Harry Farber break in horses. I used to climb up on the top rail with the others and cheer him on. He was very good with horses, and even when he was breaking them in he was a showman.

Anyhow, he noticed me sitting there and said to Frank Walsh, the manager, 'Who's that boy?'

'Oh, he belongs to George Arthur who's sinking a bore here, that kid's always running away, that's probably why he's here.'

'I wonder if he'd come with me, I'll be shorthanded and a boy could come in handy.'

'I'll drive you and the boy over this afternoon if you like. You can ask George yourself, he might let him go.'

That afternoon we all hopped in the T Model Ford and drove out to where George was still working. I stayed in the car because I was scared. I thought George would be angry with me for running away, so I wanted to avoid him.

Finally, George came over and said, 'You want to go with Farber, Jacky?'

'Yeah.' I thought it'd be fun to be with horses instead of sheep and cattle, and I was very impressed with Harry's riding.

'All right, you belong to him now', he replied. And that was that.

3

Life With Harry
1918 -1922

When we got back to the homestead Harry sent me down to Redbank, which is the main camp on Warralong. There I met Punch, a ngayarda banujutha Aborigine, and Andy Everett, a mardamarda like me. They both worked for Harry too. I slept there the night and in the morning I was given a horse and told to follow along with the others.

Harry had finished his work on Warralong and now he was heading north on his own with donkeys and horses to sell to the stations along the way. People used the horses for mustering and the donkeys for pulling wagons.

I found I was enjoying myself even though I was a bit sore from riding a horse all day. Old Punch turned out to be a nice old fella. He told me his real name was Mimirrinya, but I only called him that when we were on our own. He was very softly spoken, you could hardly hear him when he talked, but he was kind to me. Andy was good too, so all in all I was very happy. I had people talking to me and a good horse and I felt I was off on a great adventure. We covered about twenty miles that day and camped near Mardie Springs for the night.

Jimmy James was the cook, he was a whitefella and he took a shine to me. He seemed to like kids and played a bit of a game with me after tea. I was still pretty silly you see, only about thirteen at the time.

When we woke up in the morning my horse was missing. I hunted for him everywhere but couldn't find him. Harry said, 'Well, you better catch that donkey over there and ride him, or it's footleather until we find your horse!'

So I caught the donkey, it took me a while. I threw an old saddle on him and climbed on and that's when my education began. It didn't matter what I did, that donkey went where he wanted to go and it was always in the wrong direction. He'd go quiet and I'd feel pleased because I'd think he was finally settling, then he'd suddenly gallop off at full speed with me yelling and kicking and just hanging on. The others laughed and laughed when that happened, they thought it was a great joke.

Luckily for me I only had to ride him a few miles when my horse turned up. I was really glad to swap over, I decided to avoid donkeys for as long as I could after that.

When we reached China Mangroves, which is near Broome, we set up a more permanent camp. I was left there with Jimmy to feed and water some of the horses while the others continued further on with the animals that were for sale. Jimmy cooked for the both of us and during the day there wasn't much to do. At night Jimmy told me stories and answered my questions about Harry. One night I asked him how Harry came to be such a good horseman. He told me that Harry's father used to have cows and while they were being milked Harry would be riding around on the calves and getting thrown off left, right and centre. Then when he was older he graduated to horses. I could never make up my mind whether he was telling me the truth or having a joke.

Jimmy told me that Harry had made some money out of putting on buckjumping shows and challenging others to try and beat him. Between these shows he filled in his time droving, that way he had money coming in all the time.

'Listen Jacky', Jimmy said, 'I can see you're very impressed with Harry and that's all right because there's not a bareback rider that's better than him, but you watch out just the same. Stay out of his way and it'll be better for you.' I wasn't sure why he was warning me, up until then I never had any complaints about Harry. The only thing I'd noticed that I thought was a bit strange was that now and then he'd disappear for a few hours.

'Where does he go?', I asked Jimmy, 'what does he do? No one else disappears.'

'Aah women, Jacky', he said, 'they're a man's curse. Harry has a lust for the women and if he knows there are some nearby, off he goes.' I knew Jimmy must have been talking about women like my mother because there weren't any white women around.

Towards the end of three weeks Andy Everett turned up and said we were to follow him to Rollah Station as Harry had arranged to bring their cattle down to Meekatharra. Rollah was up near Lagrange Bay.

We spent a day on Rollah dipping the cattle to kill the ticks. You wouldn't want one of them to latch onto you, some were as big as threepenny bits. We stayed there a few more days while Harry organised things and then we headed back down with the cattle.

It was on the way back down that I began to realise why Jimmy had warned me. If I got in Harry's way or did anything slightly wrong he would cuff me over the ear. That was all right, but he didn't stop at that.

I was caught sneaking off and lagging behind the others so I could pick some bush fruit. Harry did his block and gave me a hiding with his stockwhip doubled up. Jimmy tried to speak up for me, but Harry wouldn't listen. He had a terrible temper and when it was roused there was no stopping him. I tried to run away that night because I had never had a hiding like that before and I was really frightened. I only got a few hundred yards when Harry noticed I was missing and came after me. I was crying and carrying on. He dragged me back to camp and gave me another hiding for running away. No one said anything. Harry was the boss and I belonged to him so he could do what he liked with me.

After that Harry would pick me up on any little thing. Once I accidentally made the cattle trot a bit fast. When he saw me later he tackled me about it and gave me a couple of hard kicks with the boot to teach me a lesson.

A couple of days later Old Punch did something wrong. I was over on the other side of the cattle so I couldn't see exactly what, but I don't think it was much. Anyway, I came round on my horse and saw Harry belting Old Punch off his horse and calling him a black bastard and so on. Punch wasn't defending himself at all, he was just letting Harry hit him. I was scared, I took off back to my spot before he got stuck into me too.

That was one thing I learnt very quickly about Harry, the only blacks he cared for were women. He'd call you Tarpot, Midnight, Charcoal, anything but your real name. He was cruel that way. Also, he liked to have a whipping boy. If I had have known that, I would have stayed with George Arthur because I was beginning to feel that station work was my real job. We had a couple of white drovers with us on the way back and if they made a mistake who did Harry take it out on? Me!

I think Harry thought twice about punching out a white bloke in case they bounced back at him. He could happily get stuck into me because I was too young to defend myself against such a big man, he was over six foot tall. And he could belt up Old Punch because he was black and it just wasn't done in those days for a blackman to best a whiteman in a fight. Punch knew that, that's why he never defended himself, because he knew it would only lead to more trouble.

We travelled day and night with those cattle. When they stopped, we stopped. When they moved, we moved. We used to sing to them a lot because they loved noise. It made them feel secure. I used to sing the corroboree songs that the old people had taught me and Harry used to sing 'I'm Going Back to Yarrawonga'. It was very hard work droving those cattle, hot and dry and dusty. I used to sleep like a log at night, I was that tired.

It was just as well I got so tired otherwise I would have lain awake worrying about dingoes. Dingoes are very cheeky. If you're riding and you've got a bit of meat or damper on you they'll come up and snap their teeth. Sometimes at night we'd chuck firesticks at them to scare them off because they were very mean animals.

Dingoes are sly. You'd think they'd run when they see you, but no, they stand there and have a real good look. Then they'll go round and try the windy side of you, they want to smell you to see if you've got something they might like to eat. It's knowing how sly they can be that makes you scared of them.

Anyway, we finally delivered the cattle to Yarlarweelor Station, that's just north-west of Peak Hill, in the Meekatharra area. The owner was Jack Matthews and he was a big, fat man and, as I was to discover, mean to boot. Harry took eighty head of cattle

Droving cattle, Murchison region, date unknown. (Battye 5458B/23)

into Meekatharra to be trucked to Perth and left me on Yarlarweelor. I soon found out that I was to be there a while as Harry was continuing on down to Perth for a holiday. Jack Matthews told me Harry would pick me up when he wanted me again, but in the meantime I belonged to him. It was 1919 by then and I was heading towards fourteen years of age.

To tell the truth, I was glad to be away from Harry. I figured Matthews couldn't be any worse. It was silly of me to think that because he came very close to it! I'd only been there a few weeks when he gave me a horse to ride but didn't tell me it was a buck jumper. He knew it would throw me, but he thought it was funny. He got his fun from doing things like that to others.

The only other person on Yarlarweelor at that time was a whiteman called Mark Mead. He was in his sixties and a nice old fella. He used to do odd jobs on the station. We were lucky because Jack left us alone a lot. He liked to go off chasing women, he was as bad as Harry in that respect.

One time he told us he was going down to Perth to pick up Ned and Toby, blackfellas, to come and work on the station. They'd belonged to another drover and he didn't want them anymore so Jack had put in for them through the Aborigines Department.

Anyway, on the way back to Yarlarweelor they ran off, maybe they'd worked out what Jack was like by then. Jack tried to track them but he wasn't much good at that sort of thing so he ended up coming back to the station and picking up me. He took me to Mt Padbury Station, where they'd been camped when they ran off.

'You follow 'em Jacky. Lose that track and you get a hiding.' I felt sorry for them, I was hoping they'd get away, but I had to track them. We passed a station mob from Mt Fraser camped at Tin Hut, which was a main camp for that station but mostly used at mustering time. Jack asked them if they'd seen two blacks. They told him that they had passed that way yesterday afternoon.

We continued to track them and finally caught up with them where some government workers were sinking a well. It was about fourteen miles from where they'd originally run away.

Jack was very, very angry by then. He ran over and grabbed them, tied one end of a rope around Toby's neck and the other around Ned's, then he gave the rope a mighty yank and sent them sprawling on the ground. The well sinkers were blasting with dynamite at the time and he sang out to them, 'You should put these two black bastards down that well and blast them too!' Then he gave them both a boot in the arse.

The well sinkers came over and offered us a cup of tea. I don't think they knew what was going on. They boiled the billy, but Jack wouldn't let them give Ned or Toby a drink.

We left after that with Ned and Toby still roped together and walking in front of us. Once we were out of sight of the well sinkers Jack stopped. He broke the limb off a mulga tree and whacked Toby over the head and made him bleed.

'You're the ringleader', he said, 'that's what you deserve!' We continued on for another three miles when he stopped again. 'Take the rope off your necks boys', he said. 'Toby, you can go, I don't want you anymore, you're just trouble. Ned, you come with me.' Toby took off, he wasn't going to hang around for another hit.

We continued on a bit further with Ned still walking in front when Jack said to me, 'This fella from Oakover, you know him?'

'No.'

'You talk Naml, see if he's really from there.'

I told Ned I was from Wanamurraganya and then I went through the names of my family and the names for all the pools, rockholes and springs in that area. They are important because a lot of family names are connected with them. After I'd been through that Ned's face lit up and he said, 'My boy, yes, you have named some of my country. I know who you are. I know your mother and your people.' It turned out he was from the Nungamarda side of that area, but there are many common words between his language and mine so he understood me easily. He told me his real name was Wilyumayinya, so I called him that when we were on our own. We continued to talk and in a few hours it was like we had known each other for years.

Jack softened up a bit after that and let Ned take turns riding my horse so he didn't have to walk all the way.

When we got back to the homestead Jack paid up Mark Mead and told him to leave. I think he figured why pay Mark when Ned could do the work for nothing.

It was shortly after that that we got into cattle-duffing or poddy-dodging as they call it. That means you pinch someone else's cattle and put your own brand on them.

There'd been a bit of rain and Jack came to us one morning and said, 'Ned, Jacky, we gotta track 'em up my cattle. They bin run away in the rain. I know their track.'

I was young and innocent, I really believed he could tell his cattle's tracks from other people's cattle.

'Jacky', he said, 'you lead 'em pack horse, catch bardis and bungarras along the way. I want to eat 'em.' He loved bungarras, he reckoned eating them was like eating butter.

We set off, and while I collected food, Ned and Jack rounded up cattle. We were out for four days and ended up with four hundred leather cleanskins. We branded them all up and then let them go. That way, when the muster was done later on, they would come in with Jack's brand on them.

After that Jack decided to go to Perth for a holiday.

'I want you to camp down the pool and catch 'em kangaroo skins when they come in for drink', he said to us. The price for roo skins was quite good at that time. 'You won't need meat, eat the roos.' He was terrible mean when it came to food. He'd gobble up a tin of tomatoes and then throw you the tin to drink from. He left us with a shotgun and one packet of cartridges, a quarter inch wire rope for roo snares, half a bag of flour, three sticks of tobacco, tea and sugar and a tin of Bullocky's Joy, that's treacle.

Ned and I set up camp near the pool to keep an eye on when the roos were coming in. Roos are fussy drinkers, they won't drink from a pool if they can dig a soak. They'll only drink from a pool if the ground is too hard and rocky for them to dig. You see, the water that comes from a soak is pure and clear with no rubbish in it.

Any nor'wester that's used to that country will dig a soak and bail it out till it comes clear. It's the best kind of water.

We cut the wire rope Jack had left to a five foot length and then unwound the strands. One strand is very strong and we ended up making over forty snares. We tied the snares to trees and heavy logs. The log has to be heavy enough so a big roo can't drag it too far. Some big boomers are very strong and they'll drag a log for miles trying to get away. The more a roo struggles with a snare the tighter it becomes.

In the morning we'd check to see how many we'd caught. You have to be quick when a roo is in a snare because they become very aggressive and want to fight you. They'll kick, bite, wrestle and hit with their tail. You've got to rush up quickly and hit them over the head with a lump of wood and put them out to it.

When Jack came back a month later we had four hundred skins baled up ready. He reckoned that was good. He was rubbing his hands and patting us on the shoulder. He took us into Meekatharra and we put the skins on the train. Skins were valuable then. Jack made a lot of money from our hard work. What did we get out of it? A quid each, that's all!

We went mustering after that with the mob from Milgun Station, which is north of Peak Hill. We all used to tend to each other's muster in those days because there were no dividing fences, so the cattle all got mixed up together. Once they were herded in, they were sorted out and each station would take what belonged to them. The only fenced paddocks then were for bullocks and horses.

The Milgun mob were a good mob and we swapped yarns as we mustered together. Suddenly, for no reason that I knew of, Jack rode alongside of me and hit me over the ear with his stockwhip. Then he grabbed me around the throat and dug his fingers in real deep and growled, 'In the Kimberleys they shoot bastards like you!'

I couldn't breathe or call out or anything. I was barely staying on my horse. I thought I was going to die.

'You bloody mongrel half-breed', he muttered, 'I can't trust you!'

Then he let me go, I was all limp and couldn't talk. There had been other blokes nearby but they never did anything. I think they were scared of him too.

It took me a while before it dawned on me why he was so angry. I talked it over with Wilyumayinya and we decided he must have thought I'd been telling the Milgun mob about the cattle-duffing we'd done earlier.

Matthews picked on me a lot after that. He'd give me hidings for not doing things right, but it wasn't my fault because he wouldn't teach me. He expected me to know how to do things I'd never done before. Once he threw me off a buggy because he reckoned I wasn't driving it the correct way. He was just a mean, hard man.

In a way I was relieved when in 1920 Jack told me Harry wanted me back.

Harry turned up and said, 'We're off north again Jacky!' That was it, no how have you been or anything like that, just, 'We're off north again Jacky!' It didn't matter how I might feel about it. If at any time I had kicked up a fuss they could have just taken me to the local policeman and he would make me do what they wanted, regardless.

Harry and I took our horses up to Roy Hill Station, picked up a herd of cattle and then brought them down to John Patrick Meehan and Sons, just out of Cue.

We went up to Beagle Bay then just with our plant and work horses. That took about a month, it's a long trip and rough country. Dingo Dan, the cook, and I were made to stay camped at Boans Well, which is just this side of Broome, while Harry and the other men continued on through rough country to pick up some cattle to bring back down.

Dingo Dan's real name was Dan Mattocks, but everyone called him Dingo Dan because in his spare time he worked for himself chasing dingoes. It was good money then, the government supplied the strychnine, and you were your own boss to boot. Dan was a fat fella, he loved cooking and eating and you always got a good meal with him around.

Harry and the boys returned to us in three weeks with five hundred head of cattle and extra men to help with the droving. He called in at Broome gaol and picked up two Mulbas that he had promised a policeman he would bring down to Meekatharra. Jack McMahon was with us on that trip. When he got his own plant later everyone called him Jack the Roarer, because he used to yell all the time. I had a few run-ins with him but he never ended up belting me. As for Harry, well he was still the same in every respect. His latest was grabbing you by the ears and shaking you, he hadn't changed at all.

On the trail about four days ahead of us was another droving mob. We passed Crofton's Camp, where they had stayed, a few days later and to my surprise I saw sitting on the flat under a tree a shirt, trousers and Ashburton hat. I picked up the hat and put it on, it fitted all right so I wore it. I took the clothes too, there were one or two specks of blood on the shirt but I never thought anything of it at the time. We drove along a few more days when we saw this buggy and pair coming towards us, it was Detective Sergeant Manning and I think Frank Growden, a policeman, from Nullagine. They had Kimberley blacktrackers with them. They talked to Harry and told him that someone had been murdered in the mob ahead of us and they were looking for the body. I started to feel real funny about those clothes then. I had a real strong feeling they belonged to a dead man.

A couple of days later they caught up with us again. They had found the body and had it tied under the buggy, wrapped in a bag.

A friend of mine had been with that mob and he told me the full story later. He said their boss, Jack Parkes, had been a terrible mean man, with that Kimberley whiteman mentality. What I mean by that is, he thought he could do what he liked with a blackman.

46

A lot of men who lived in the Kimberleys thought like that in those days. They classed the blackman the same as a dog.

Anyhow, the boss picked a fight with Bobby, a young fella from the Kimberleys, and without thinking Bobby defended himself and won the fight. He bested the boss and that just wasn't done.

The next day the boss sent the others on and kept Bobby with him. He made him take his clothes off, they were the ones I found, and then he walked him to the top of a quartz hill and shot him and left the body there unburied. Later the police arrested Jack Parkes down near Ethel Creek and tied him to the verandah of the homestead because there was no lock-up there. Then they sent word to Detective Sergeant Manning who came up with the trackers in the buggy and pair to look for the body.

Poor old Bobby, he was only twenty-eight when he died and he was only shot because he was black and a whiteman thought he could get away with it. I heard that Jack Parkes got two years' gaol.

When we hit Roy Hill with the cattle we stopped there a while to pick up a fresh mob to take down to John Patrick Meehan and Sons on Austin Downs Station just out of Cue.

On the way to Cue we camped at Number 38 Well, which is about halfway between Roy Hill and Meekatharra. That was when Harry outdid himself as far as women go.

We were camped there having a bit of a break when two tribal women walked in and went up to Harry on the cart and asked for some tea and sugar. He talked to them for a couple of minutes and the next thing Punch and Andy were nudging me and saying, 'Look, look, he's going to have woman!' We were only a hundred yards away and could see Harry taking his trousers off. He had one and then he had the other, right there in broad daylight in front of the cattle and us. He had no shame.

I suppose I shouldn't single him out really, there were plenty of men like that in those days. They thought that's all black women were good for.

Anyway, we delivered that mob to Austin Downs and then went into Cue for a bit of a break. We camped down at the trucking yards which were situated between Daydawn and Cue, and went into Cue for some entertainment. Of course there wasn't much for

47

me to do so I spent my time watching the others get rotten drunk. Then they'd all start fighting with one another, those whitefellas were terrible the way they hit the booze.

We were there for a week and then Harry decided we'd go out chasing brumbies. We did that for a month. The next thing I heard Harry was getting married, I think she was a girl he'd known for a while and he finally decided to tie the knot. She was a nice girl, a fair bit younger than him though. I think she wanted Harry to settle down because he took a job on managing Mt Fraser Station and I had to go with him.

It wasn't like Harry to settle in one place, he liked the wide open spaces too much. I stayed on Mt Fraser for about a year doing whatever jobs Harry gave me. Rita, Harry's wife, didn't like it much. She was the only white woman and there weren't many visitors so I suppose she got lonely. Harry ended up leaving Mt Fraser and moving into Meekatharra to live. He left me on the station and said when he wanted me he'd come back.

In 1922 he sent word to Mt Fraser that he was giving up town life and going back droving and I was to get a lift with 'Banjo' Patterson, and meet him at Roy Hill. 'Banjo' Patterson had an old Dodge car and trailer and used to do the mail run between Marble Bar and Meekatharra.

When 'Banjo' came through I loaded my riding gear and swag onto his trailer and off we went. Besides me, he was giving a lift to Charlie Alcorn, an old-time drover, and an old white lady, whose name I don't know.

It was dark fairly soon and every time the car headlights hit the river gums it made them stand out really white against the night. The old lady noticed this and kept commenting, 'Ooh, look at those lovely white trees Mr Alcorn, how do they get them so white?'

This was too much for Charlie, who loved to spin a yarn whenever he could, so he replied, 'Yes, we've got nigger boys up here, little fellows they are. We give them kerosene tins cut in half and filled with white paint. It's their job to paint those trees so they stay white.'

'Oh yes', she said, 'well they certainly do a good job'.

Charlie could hardly stop himself from laughing. He told me

48

later she was a lady from Perth and not used to the north.

I had first come across Charlie Alcorn around 1919, he was well-known for his tall stories, but the one that was my favorite was this one. He was out droving and camped near a beach. During the night the cattle stampeded into the water and started swimming out to sea. Charlie hopped on his horse and tried to stop them, but the horse went into the water as well. Pretty soon the sharks were coming in for what they thought was a free feed, so what did he do? He jumped from his horse onto the shark's back and shepherded all the other sharks out to sea. 'Yes Jacky', he said, 'it's amazing what a man will do to protect his cattle!'

Harry picked me up at Roy Hill as promised and we went up to De Grey where we picked up five thousand sheep and moved out towards Muccan Station.

The eclipse of the sun was on then and there was a great interest in it. On Wallal Downs Station, which is situated between Broome and Port Hedland, they had big telescopes set up and scientists from all over the world were there waiting to see it. You were supposed to get a really good view of it from Wallal. Anyway, it didn't seem to bother the sheep too much and I was prepared for it because the cook who was with us had told me all about it from what he had read in the paper. 'Going to be an eclipse Jacky, it'll go dark for a while and then come good again. Nothing to be scared of.' So you see, I knew what to expect.

By the time we reached Muccan Station I had taken it into my head to try and rid myself of Harry once and for all. I was sick of being his whipping boy and I was getting on for seventeen years old now and felt I could take care of myself. That night, after all the sheep had been yarded, I went down to where the old people were camped and had a talk to them. Paddy Ball, another mardamarda, was there too.

'Where are you fellas going?', I asked. I knew they were on the move.

'Going pink-eye* tomorrow', they said.

---

* Pink-eye: a term used by the Aboriginal people of North West Australia, similar to the more widely known term 'walkabout'. It designates a period of wandering as a nomad, often as undertaken by Aborigines who feel the need to leave the place where they are in contact with white society and return to their traditional way of life. Can also simply mean a holiday, usually taken without leave.

'Well, I'm going too', I told them.

'If you're going, I'm going', said Paddy. 'I'm sick of drovers! We better get up bloody early though, otherwise someone might see us.'

Paddy and I sneaked off at first light. The old people caught up with us about six miles out. We moved on and camped, then moved on again. I was looking over my shoulder all the way, thinking any minute Harry might turn up. I looked and looked, but he never came. Maybe he was sick of me too.

Finally, I headed towards Bungalow Station because I had been told that my Aunty Nellie and Clancy McKenna were there and I was anxious to see them. I felt that at last I had a little bit of freedom. I wanted to be able to do as I pleased without the boot being put in for every little mistake. I wanted to be independent and not have to follow a whiteman around all the time. I wanted to make something of my life.

4

A Man In The Mulba Way
1922-1923

Aunty was really excited to see me, she recognised me straight away, and it was wonderful to be with Clancy McKenna again. I hadn't seen him for a while. He was a few years younger than me and our lives would go in different directions, but we would always be close, seeing each other when we could and swapping yarns and stories.

Aunty got me work on Bungalow to tide me over because I had no money or tucker. Conditions there were pretty much the same as the other stations. No wages, take your stale bread and meat to the woodheap to eat.

The worst thing there was the tea. In those days tea was a nor'wester's life-blood. Boiling the billy and having a drink of tea with plenty of sugar was what kept you going. On Bungalow they had a kerosene bucket next to the stove on the floor, the white people emptied their old tea leaves in it. Then the cook stewed it all up again and gave it to us to drink. It tasted bloody awful. The only time you got a decent mug was when you were out bush and there was no second-hand stuff around.

I was on Bungalow for five months when the work started to cut out. It was corroboree time and a lot of my mates and relatives were gathering on Bungalow. One of them was Wuruwurunyu, or Donkey Charlie, he was like a brother to me in the Aboriginal way, because there was a common grandmother somewhere. He was a close relation to me, the next closest to my brother Jimmy when it came to men's business. That's how the old people thought of it anyway.

It's hard for white people to understand because they have different family relationships. We can call someone a close relation who a white person wouldn't think was close at all. I'd call my cousins brothers, because that's how I think of them. We don't just go on blood relationships, but on skin groups, and the old grannies. So it's a different set up altogether. It's very hard to explain. I used to try and explain it to white people who asked me but now I just refuse. I get too frustrated with the whole thing because their minds think a different way. Let's just say that Wuruwurunya was close to me in my people's terms.

What I didn't know then was that Wuruwurunya had been to see my brother Jimmy, and some of my aunties and grannies, to get permission to put me through the Law. My brother was far away at the time and couldn't arrange it himself so he agreed to let Wuruwurunya take charge of me. If I had have known what was going on behind the scenes I'd have left quick.

We were all sitting around the fire one night swapping yarns when they grabbed me. They sneaked up and put a hair-belt around my waist and said, 'You got to stay with us now, we go tomorrow to get your doctors'.

I didn't argue, I just gave in to them. When you've had that hair-belt put around you, you're very silly to run away because it makes it worse when they catch you.

I think they might have been a bit worried that I might make a run for it because they stayed close to me all night, guarding me like a mob of policemen!

The women cried and wailed on and off that night, especially the old grannies, they're the worst, they go on and on. They do that because they know their boy is going to suffer and there's nothing they can do about it. If they could, they would spare you the pain, but they know they can't.

We left early the next morning and walked over to Ettrick Station which is about fifteen miles away. That afternoon I was taken out bush and had Law songs sung over me. The following morning we left Ettrick with forty men and walked over to Mullyie Station where they sang more songs and gathered more men.

Then they dressed me up like a wild blackfella. No clothes, just

52

paint, feathers, leaves, and anything you might find in the bush. I was rigged up as a marlurlu, that means a young man about to be circumcised. I still had my hair-belt on, that's very important. It has the importance of Ngarrga which is God. It's like being baptised is in some religions.

The following day they took me down to see the station manager on Mullyie so that he understood an important ceremony was about to take place and would give permission for everyone to leave and go to Warralong for the big corroboree. When they showed me to him he said, 'Yes, I can see what's going on, you can take the men and whoever you need and go'.

We reached Redbank on Warralong the next day and found between four and five hundred people waiting. The word had gone out and they had been coming from all over the place. My ceremony was to be the following morning. At first light they started singing the Law songs which tell people the ceremony is coming soon. Then when those are finished, it's time.

Some of the men hold your arms, legs and chest, and they cover your mouth so you can't scream. It's very painful, but it's not too long before it's over.

You always have more than one doctor. I had five, but I've met others who've had up to fifteen. Not everyone does the cutting, but it has the same significance. It means all those men are obligated to look after you if you ever meet them again. That's why they like to get men who are out of your home area, because if you ever leave your country and go into theirs, you have a relation who will look after you.

You don't always know who your doctors are because they don't tell you. You might be in a strange country one day and a man will come up and lay a shirt or food at your feet, then he'll hug you. It's only in that moment that you know he was one of your doctors.

Of course, some are better doctors than others but it's all very clean and neat. They use a very sharp stone flint and they put bush medicine on it afterwards called gardil gardil, it comes from a grey bush with banana shaped leaves and helps to dry out the wound.

Before, during and after the ceremony the songs are going on and they have great importance. They are secret songs that the women aren't allowed to hear. No one can date those songs. There is no living memory of them ever being invented. No one can say their great, great grandfather made up those songs because they have always existed. They were made by God, not man. That's why they are so special.

I was kept on Warralong for two days and then moved back to Bungalow Station where they made a permanent hospital for me there. For two weeks they kept me out in the bush surrounded by devil-devil sticks for protection.

Altogether, from the time they first put the hair-belt on me, to when I was finished in the bush hospital, it was three weeks. I've known others who've been kept away for five weeks. During this time I heard many new songs and stories and other men tried to help me understand the Law.

When it was all over I was allowed to join my family again. The women all cry and carry on when you come in because they have lost their child but they're also happy for you because your suffering is over.

They tease you and say, 'You can have nyuba* now!' That means you can have a woman because you're a man now. I was supposed to have Billy Moses' sister but she was already with someone else. She was willing to come to me but I said no because, to tell you the truth, I'd only just got my freedom. I was worried that if I got mixed up with a woman I might get tied down again.

We all left Bungalow then and went pink-eye to Yarrie Station. There were more meetings there and corroborees. I thought they might do Clancy McKenna, but they decided to leave him. For the first few days there we lived mainly on pie melon. We used to cut them in half, take the seeds out, turn them upside down in the hot sand and cover them with ashes. They take less than an hour to cook. After three days of melon we were all starving for meat. Luckily, someone caught an emu. We were very poorly treated then, it was hard for us just to live.

That was a wonderful time for me, to be with my family, to

* Nyuba: A person who is the correct tribal relationship to another person for the purpose of marriage. (Also spelt 'nuba'.)

sit around the campfire at night and hear the stories and songs of the old people. It reminded me of when I was young and my Uncle Hector used to sit me on his knee. It reminded me of my mother and her singing. It reminded me of all the things I had left behind when I had been given to whitemen.

I remember two stories from that time, I will tell them to you.

The first is about two sisters, they were more or less twins. They used to wander around on their own from waterhole to waterhole, with no man to look after them or keep them company.

One day this fella came along. He saw these two women and wondered what they were for because he'd never seen women before. Maybe they devil-devil he thought, but as he looked at them he thought, no, they not devil-devil. The more he looked the curiouser he got, until finally he sang out and got their attention.

'Don't come any closer', they said. 'You're not allowed to. You can only talk to us from your own place.'

Now according to the laws of the people, he wasn't supposed to be talking to them or approaching them directly at all because they were tua to him. That means if they had a daughter, they would give her to him to be his nyuba. When someone is tua, you don't muck around with them.

The women camped in their spot for the night and the man made his camp further away. In the morning he rose early and went to a nearby rockhole where he caught some birds and marsupials to eat. He put some out for the women then backed off to his own camp because they wouldn't come and collect it until he was well out the way. They took the food and cooked it and then put some out for him, but he wasn't allowed to collect it until they were back in their own camp.

This went on for a few days until the man started to have ideas about those women. Ooh yes, he was thinking a lot! Ooh yes, he could think of something they might be good for! I think he wanted to get close to them as quickly as possible.

One night he laid down and pretended he was going to sleep. He had a plan.

'Goodnight', he called out to the women in a shy sort of way. He knew what he was doing all right!

Suddenly, he made a yakii.

'Yakii', he called, 'yakii!!'

The women heard him and called out, 'What's the matter?'

'Oh, ants bitin' me', he said.

So they told him, 'Come a bit closer'.

He moved a bit closer, and in his heart he's gettin' gladder and gladder!

Suddenly, he made another yakii.

'Yakii, yakii!', he shouted.

'What's the matter now?', the women asked.

'Oh ants here too, they still bitin' me!'

So once more they said, 'Come a bit closer then'.

He moved closer.

He carried on like this until finally they said, 'Look, come and sleep just the other side of our fire, you'll be all right there'.

Ooh, he thought that was really good, not far to go now. He settled down there and for a while he was as happy as can be, but suddenly he leapt up and started yelling, 'YAKII! YAKII! YAKII! Ants terrible here! They bitin' real hard.'

'How is it that you've got all the ants? We haven't got any', one of the sisters said.

'I don't know', he said, 'but they terrible!'

Finally, the other sister said, 'You come and lay between us, then the ants won't bite you'. Ooh by gee he thought that was wonderful. He was real glad now.

Of course the game was on then! He had his arms all round them and he's singin' and singin' about how this is the greatest thing that's ever happened in the world.

The next morning at piccaninny daylight he went out hunting again. He wanted to keep those women happy. He caught six bungarras, but while he was away the sisters decided to leave because they knew they were tua to him so the relationship was wrong.

When this fella came back he was real upset. He tracked them and tracked them until finally he caught up with them. They had climbed on top of a hill and were just sitting there.

'What are you doin'?', he asked real friendly.

'Sittin' here', they said.

He tried to get up to them but he couldn't because the way

56

was too slippery. The women made it that way using magic. He talked to them and talked to them, but they wouldn't come down. They told him they didn't want to have anything to do with him.

Now one sister had very long hair and the other had a firestick. Every time the one with the long hair leaned over, the man would grab hold and try to climb up, but he never got very far because the sister with the firestick would burn the hair off. This went on for a very long time. That man just wouldn't give up because he was mad for those women.

Finally, after many tries, he dropped down dead. The moment he died, the two sisters turned into twin peaks. You can still see them today on the way out to the Woody Woody manganese mine. They are on the flat and there are no other hills near them. That's a very old story.

The second story is not really a story, it's more talk about the gulingguras, or pixies, as white people call them.

There's a special place not far from Bonnie Downs where at sundown you can see through a bit of a hole in a hill. It's considered a special place because a lot of gulingguras are supposed to live there in the caves. They are male and female, they don't wear clothes and they are very small. I don't know what their purpose is, I suppose they are just part of the world, the same as we are. I do know this though, they like to be left alone. They don't like people hanging around in their area.

Anyway, the old people used to sing a song about them, and whenever they sang it to us young blokes we used to get so scared we could feel the hair sticking up on the backs of our necks, and we would almost imagine that we could see gulingguras in the firelight.

The song tells how you're sitting by yourself near a pool in the Nullagine area, which is known to have gulingguras. It's very dark and very quiet. You start to feel a little bit nervous, just a little bit. Then your stomach starts playing up and you get a little bit frightened there too. You try and make yourself feel better but all the time you're slowly getting more and more frightened, until finally you're terrified because you know it hasn't just been your imagination. You know there are gulingguras all around you in the dark. You're surrounded, you can see their eyes and their teeth flash in the moonlight. You can feel them creeping closer and closer and closer. You want to get up and run away but you can't because you're frozen.

You see, we were all taught to be frightened of gulingguras because no one has ever found out exactly what they like to eat.

Those old people were wonderful storytellers. Some of the stories they told me I've forgotten now. I think they used to enjoy scaring us, it gave them a lot of fun.

Even though I was a man now it didn't mean I was entitled to the knowledge of everything. There was a further stage of the Law which I should have gone through but I didn't. It was compulsory for the young men who were ngayarda banujuthas, but at that time they weren't worrying about it too much for us mardamardas. Most of us were being taken away and put in missions and settlements. We weren't allowed to spend much time with our tribal people so this interfered with what they'd like to do with us.

Part of it was to do with whether you were allowed to see certain sacred sites or not. It cost a lot to see a sacred site then. Just because you'd been initiated didn't automatically mean you could go there. There were other ceremonies that put you further into the Law and gave you more status in the old people's eyes. It meant dressing up in your wild-life gear again and going out into the bush for three or four days and not returning until you had caught as many kangaroos, bungarras and emus as you could.

When you were ready to come back in you had to carry three roos on your head. They were cooked, and split down the middle so they could be carried easily. All that food was a heavy load to carry. You have to take it into the camp and lay it in front of the old people just like they were kings. It was only after that that they might show you the site.

A sacred site could be a cave, a rock, a pool, anywhere where a big snake could be or where he comes now and then. I'm not talking about a real snake in the sense of something you can see, I'm talking about a very old spiritual thing. I suppose a white person's sacred site might be his church, but you know when that church was built and you can feel it with your hands. Our sacred sites are more to do with the spirits, and they can't be dated because they've always been there.

58

There used to be a sacred site on the way back from the Comet mine, which is about six miles south-west of Marble Bar. Just as you drive over the point of a big hill, there used to be a little bit of a creek that ran under a gum tree. It had been there for hundreds and hundreds and hundreds of years. When I was young you could always count on getting a drink of water there, even in drought time.

Unfortunately, white people didn't understand how special this place was. Someone went and dug a hole there, probably a prospector, hoping the water would build up, but of course it didn't, it just died away. You see, in doing that he killed Gadagadara, a snake with a strange head shaped like a horse's, who had placed his spirit there to live and keep the water for the people.

I remember the old ones being very upset when that site was destroyed. They had a meeting to try and work out who had killed Gadagadara, but no one knew. They were very sad for a long time after that.

There have been a number of places like that where I come from. In these special places there's been water, sometimes just a puddle, and then someone sends a grader in or someone tampers with it, and of course the water disappears because the spirit that kept it has been killed.

There are other things, sacred objects, which you also have to pay to see. These things are hidden around the area in special places and are used in Law ceremonies. Once again, only the old people know where they are kept and it is only they who give permission for a man to see them.

The old ones believe there's a great deal of supernatural power stored in these instruments. That's why they are so careful with them. If a young fella or a woman accidentally saw them, they'd die.

Sometimes you get some silly idiot who deliberately sets out to see them thinking he can fool the old people, but the old ones have their ways of knowing what someone's been up to. For example, if you leave a track, they can tell who made it, man or woman, what age, their name. They are very clever that way. When they know who it is they go straight up to that person and tell them they want to see them at a certain place and time, and that's when they get them. They might make them drink Yamarli creeper crushed up in tea or water, that's poisonous, or they might kill them maban way. You can't fool the old people!

In all of these things, the old people aren't just the guardians of the Law, they are the Law, alive.

5

Camel Teams And Station Work
1923-1924

When pink-eye was finished at Yarrie Station I said goodbye to
my Aunty Nellie and Clancy McKenna and headed for Marble Bar.
Now I was free I was determined to spend some time with my
Aunty Dinah and Jack Doherty and the old people there. I knew
Aunty was working at the Marble Bar Hospital, cooking and cleaning,
and my Aunty Fanny was working for the postmaster, so I was
looking forward to seeing them both.

I walked down to the Coongan Pub and grabbed a train. Before
I knew it I was in the Bar and looking for my relatives straight
away. They cried when they saw me, they wailed and wailed, they
were that pleased to have me back.

'You a man now Jacky', they said, and they were cryin' and laughin'.
Mulbas are great ones for teasing you.

To my surprise Jack's brother, Clancy Doherty, had returned
from Perth and was in the Bar too. I was really pleased to meet
him. He had a job with the Afghans driving camel teams, and
who was his offsider but my friend, Billy Moses. It was a happy
reunion all round.

I'd only been in the Bar three days when who should turn up
but my brother Jimmy Watson. He'd been working at Wallareenya
Station and had been keeping tabs on me through the Mulba
grapevine. He wanted to see me now I'd been through the Law.
Jimmy could only stay a few days but during that time we talked
and talked and the five of us were very spoilt by the aunties.

It was after Jimmy left that Jack started pestering his mother

61

about my father. I had always thought it was Sandy McPhee. No one had ever told me that, it was just that he took an interest in me, so I assumed he was. I think Jack must have suspected something or he wouldn't have taken it up with Aunty. 'Who is it really Mum?' he kept asking, 'who's his father?'

Finally she said, 'Bert Watson'.

I felt shocked, and angry too. The squatters and the storekeepers, they were always innocent. But if they were so good, then tell me this, where did all us mardamarda people come from?

'Tell him about it Mum', Jack went on. I wanted to leave it right there and then but Jack went on and on. Finally Aunty told me.

'Well, Jacky. Your Mum worked for him in the store, that's how you come to be. But when you were born and he saw you weren't tribal like Jimmy, he kicked you all out. He didn't want no one to know you were his kid, but your Mum, she know. Sandy McPhee took you in then, he was a good man, but he not your father.'

'Now you know', Jack said. I wasn't feeling very happy about knowing just then. In fact, I was angry with Jack for bringing it up. I think I'd rather have kept to Sandy than know about that other bastard!

I haven't told many people about Bert Watson being my father. I figured if he didn't want me then I didn't want him. I wasn't even going to put him in this book, but I'm old now and it doesn't seem to matter so much anymore. Also, that kind of business went on all the time up North, white men having our mothers and then not owning up to the results, I think it's time people knew about these things.

I'd been in the Bar a few weeks when one day Billy Thompson, who owned the blacksmith's shop, sang out to Jack, 'Who's your mate?'

Jack told him who I was and where I belonged.

'Will he take a job?', Billy asked, 'he can go out with my sons Alf and Sandy, delivering goods to stations'. Thompsons and the Afghans serviced all the stores and stations in the area, delivering food and goods, picking up wool and so on. I knew I'd have to get a job sooner or later, so I agreed.

Thompsons were very good to work for. They were fair, fed me good tucker, and gave me a bit of money as well. You have to remember that wages were very poor in those days, nothing like what you get now. Of course, goods were cheaper too. You could get a shirt and trousers for seven shillings and sixpence and a full rig out, a complete suit, only cost one pound if you were small, and a bit more if you were big. There was a Chinese tailor in the Bar then, you could go to his place at eight in the morning and he would measure you up and by five in the afternoon you could pick up your suit. The Chinese laundryman was good too. Later, when Jack and I had bought a good set of clothes each, we would take them to him and he would wash and iron them for two shillings.

Alf Thompson and I got on well together, they were a nice family. In the morning we would get up early, hunt up the camels, bring them in and harness them. Then we'd have breakfast, which could be anything from bread and tea to left over stew from the night before. Whatever it was, we cleaned it up real quick.

After that we'd be off, delivering and picking up goods from whatever station wanted us. I had to do a lot of walking on those long trips. Around Marble Bar there's some very rough, hilly country and in those days the tracks were quite steep. I had to walk behind the wagon ready to pull the brake on quickly if it was needed. Coming down a steep hill I had to pull it on all the time, it was very slow going, but the only safe way to travel.

I'll never forget the time the wagon got away from us. We were coming back into the Bar loaded up with wool bales and perched on the top was a swaggy we'd picked up. Sandy Thompson was ahead of us with another wagon. Fortunately, he was nearly to the bottom of the hill before we got into trouble, otherwise it might have been a different story.

Halfway down the hill our wagon began to pick up speed, so Alf sang out. 'Pull the brake on!'

I was running behind by that stage pulling the brake on all the time but it wouldn't grip. I realised then that the screw that held it in place had been completely stripped and there was no grip left. I sang out to Alf, 'Brake's gone!', and he yelled to the swaggy on top, 'Jump you stupid bugger, jump while you can'.

The swaggy wasn't going to jump, the wagon was going too fast by then. He was hanging on for dear life.

Sandy looked up and saw us hurtling down the hill, he quickly started to move his wagon out the way. We flew past with only inches between us. Once our wagon hit level ground it slowed down and Alf was finally able to pull up.

We had been very, very lucky. It would have only needed one of those camels to trip and the whole wagon would have gone over. That's one thing about camels, they are very sure-footed animals.

Whenever Alf, Sandy and I came in after a long haul old Mrs Thompson would always have a good meal waiting for us. She was a very good cook and fed me the same food she fed her sons. There was no eating on the woodheap either, we ate at the table in the dining-room. Thompsons were very good that way.

I remember one morning, we hadn't been back long and Alf and I were sitting having a smoko near Billy's blacksmith shop when the parson came along and said, 'Good morning Mr Thompson'.

'Good morning parson, nice morning.'

'Yes, a lovely morning Mr Thompson. You know, a very strange thing happened this morning. I was in the church when my pet Magpie flew in and landed on the cross, I've never seen him do that before. Then he started singing Home Sweet Home. He sang his little heart out. In fact, he sang so hard that some muck flew out of his bottom in the shape of a cross.'

Well old Billy didn't grin or bat an eyelid. He just looked straight at the parson and said, 'It must be a funny day parson, because this morning my Butcher bird flew in and landed on my anvil. Then he started singing Home Sweet Home, the same as your Magpie. He sang so hard that sparks shot out of his arse!'

Alf and I laughed and laughed, Billy had gotten the best of the parson. That's one thing you can say about nor'westers, they love a good story.

There was another funny thing that happened when we were on a break from the delivery run. I'll tell you about it.

Charlie was an old tribal bloke who worked for Billy Thompson. Billy wasn't only the blacksmith, he was in charge of the rubbish run too. He used to send Charlie around with a horse and cart to collect the rubbish. The horse's name was also Charlie.

Anyway, one day Charlie set off and his first stop was the police station.

'Charlie', said the policeman, 'there's a lot of flies round Charlie's collar, is he all right?' They had a look and saw that the horse's neck was rubbed raw and infected.

'You can't cart rubbish with him like this. Take him back to Billy and get him to put him in the stable and do something with him.' So Charlie did that.

The next day the policeman came down to see Billy about the horse. Charlie was sitting just outside the shop having a smoko. The policeman went in and said, 'Listen Billy, I wanted to talk to you privately rather than in front of the whole town, I've been thinking about Charlie, it'd be best to take him down to the gully and shoot him.'

'Yes, I think you're right. He's getting too old to be of much use anymore.'

Well, old Charlie didn't finish his tea, he just left it standing there. He got up and walked slowly down to the cover of some tea trees. Then he followed the creek and headed off towards the Coongan. He wasn't seen in the area again for fifteen years.

When Alf and I were out on the road we would often travel in convoy with the Afghan teams. Most of the Afghans earned their living transporting goods. They'd carry anything except bacon, or anything that had been in contact with bacon. It was against their religion. Some people respected this and some didn't.

I remember once when I was giving Nick Mohomet a hand, we pulled into the store and Nick said, 'I'm here to pick up some oats, Mr Martin'. Martin's nickname was the White Bull because of the way he carried on with the women.

Anyhow, Martin went inside to get the oats and for some reason he couldn't get them onto the back of the wagon quick enough. This made Nick suspicious so he leapt up and checked the bag. The White Bull had put the oats inside a bacon bag. Nick was furious. He threw it onto the ground and shouted, 'You can keep your dirty, rotten oats!'

It was mean to do that because it was in their agreement that they didn't have to carry anything to do with bacon. I think their religion should have been respected.

The Afghans were wonderful companions to have on a trip. They had a different routine to us. They never pulled up for lunch or to boil a billy or anything like that. Instead they would keep

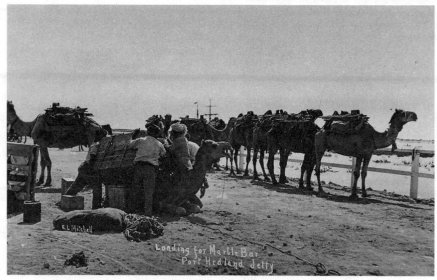

Afghans loading Camels, Port Hedland, 1919. (Battye 641B/5)

themselves going with flapjacks. They were like giant pancakes that never went hard. They'd roll them up and keep them inside their tunic and eat them when they got hungry.

At night we'd all camp together and the Afghans would make a giant curry. When it was ready they would offer it to us first. We'd go over and help ourselves to as much as we wanted, we used to really pile our plates high because they were very good cooks. When we'd all finished getting our share they'd have a bit of a prayer, then wash their lips and fingers. Then they would sit round the curry and eat with their fingers from that one big bowl. That was their custom.

They were very generous, you couldn't wish for better people. They wouldn't let you walk past without offering you something to eat or drink. Often when I was on my breaks in the Bar I would go down to their camp with Clancy and Jack, who was also working for them by then, because they were so friendly and kind. Of course, they liked their share of women too, but they treated them better, and provided for the kids that came along, not like the squatters and some of the policemen round there.

Sometimes, the women would be gaoled overnight for no good

reason. It was so the policeman could have a go. You couldn't do much about that kind of thing in those days. Who were you going to complain to, the police? Also, the women liked to keep that kind of business to themselves. Some of them thought it a big shame, others didn't want to say anything in case they got gaoled again.

All in all, the Afghans got on very well with the Aboriginal people. It's hard to explain, but they were more like us. They didn't class us worse than them, they classed us the same.

I ended up working for Thompsons for about eighteen months and during that time I developed a respect not only for Afghans but for camels as well. You don't have to worry about camels the way you do other animals. You don't have to shoe them or buy them bran and oats. You can give them one drink and then use them for a week without watering them. They're good workers, you can use them to pull wagons, pack them or ride them. They're beautiful to ride on once you get used to them. I had a camel called Alice, she used to rock me to sleep she was so gentle.

I left Thompsons in the end only because I was sick of walking. I was just a silly young fella who didn't know when he was well off. I decided I wanted a bit more excitement in my life and I couldn't see myself getting it walking behind a wagon for miles and miles.

I went out to Limestone to see if I could get a job there because Tommy Mallett, the owner, was well-known for being the best squatter in the area. Also, I knew some of my mates were out there, Billy Moses, Clancy McKenna, Dougall and so on. They were all blackfellas.

Tommy took one look at me and gave me a job straight away. He was known for being a fair man, he fed you well, and he'd trust you on a job instead of standing over you like some others did. We only had to work till midday Saturday and we got Sunday off. Tommy used to have a kill on Tuesdays, get the butcher in Wednesday and then cook it all up into curry and Irish stew for us. He built a dining hall, which was meant to be for blacks and whites alike. He wanted the blacks to eat in there with the whitemen but they wouldn't because they felt uncomfortable. They thought it was a big shame to eat with the whitefellas. I used to eat in there, it never worried me, but a lot of the others used to eat outside on the woodheap!

In the fifteen months I was there I really enjoyed myself. It was good to be with my friends and relatives. It was wonderful to be with Clancy McKenna again. Even though we were both mardamardas we had led very different lives, because I had spent nearly all my time with white people while he had stayed with his mother and spent all his time with the real Mulbas. It would lead us in different directions later on, but we would always be close to one another.

Towards the end of my time there Tommy hired Joe Exton as manager. Limestone was running both sheep and cattle at that time and it was hard to get a man who knew how to handle both. Joe was all right, but he liked to work us harder than Tommy. We found that out when Tommy went to Perth for a holiday and left him in charge. We worked long hours, and all day Saturday and sometimes Sunday too. We got a bit sick of it.

Now, at that time Hubert Brockman was managing Corunna Downs for Howden Drake-Brockman, and he and his wife and Helen Bunda, a mardamarda, used to come over now and then and spend weekends at Limestone. Hubert was friends with Joe Exton. Helen was a very attractive girl, but I knew she was supposed to be promised to Albert Brockman, so I kept my distance.

One Saturday night after tea Joe called me over and said, 'Jack how would you like to take Minbaringu over to Corunna? That old man of hers is ill-treating her. Also, Hubert needs a man to work for him at Top Camp.'

Now it was true that her husband used to beat her every time he caught her talking to a young fella, he was a very jealous man. However, Joe was having her too and I think he wanted to get her over to Corunna so he could visit her on weekends without worrying about it causing trouble.

I wasn't that fussed about going, but they were very keen for me to go. I wanted to stay in good with them and I didn't want to lose my job, so I agreed.

'Good! Go and see the cook', said Hubert when I said I'd do it, 'get some tea, sugar, flour and meat. You can leave tonight.'

We walked five miles that night before we camped. I made sure we camped on a rise just in case we were being followed. There was twenty-five miles overland between Corunna and Limestone and I was anxious to cover that ground without any trouble. You see, what Joe didn't realise was that I shouldn't be doing what I'd agreed to do. Minbaringu belonged to old Billy by Law. Even though he wasn't good to her she was still his. Also, her relationship to me was straight nyuba, which made it even worse because the people would think I had an interest in her that way.

When we finally arrived at the Corunna homestead, Hubert had a horse and sulky waiting. 'Hop in and go to Top Camp', he said, 'stay there until I contact you just in case her blacks have followed her up and there's trouble'. Top Camp was sixteen miles from the Corunna homestead. It turned out we had been followed by fourteen Mulbas, but Hubert threatened them with the police and hunted them off with the rifle.

Later, Minbaringu returned from Top Camp to be a housegirl and sure enough, Joe began visiting on weekends.

There was a lot of work for me to do at Top Camp. Hubert Brockman had just fired Peter Link, who had worked on Corunna for years. Peter had lost his temper and smashed things up. He'd broken the blacksmith's anvil and damaged some windmills and things like that.

Peter had lived with black women for years and years. There was only one kid he owned up to, and he called him Peter, so I suppose that was good of him. One day someone suggested to Peter that he teach his kid how to read and write, so he could make something of himself when he grew up.

'No fear', said Peter, 'keep them as they are, otherwise they might end up knowing too bloody much. Why, they could even end up knowing more than you and me and that wouldn't be right!'

A lot of people thought like that then. The idea was to keep us in our place, whatever that was. If I'd been offered it, I'd have grabbed a chance at an education with both hands.

I stayed in Top Camp for about twelve months, fixing sheep yards and windmills. Corunna was sold to Foulkes-Taylor and Hubert and his family left for Portree Station and took Helen Bunda with them. Joe Exton came over as manager then and I went down to the homestead and became Foulkes-Taylor's offsider.

6

Corunna Downs Station
1924-1927

Foulkes-Taylor was a hard man. Of course, he'd been to War, and that makes a man hard. He worked very hard himself and he expected everyone else to do the same. All he thought about was work and more work, and he was very fussy about how things were done. For example, one time he asked me to dig a posthole.

'I want it three feet deep', he told me, 'sing out when you've done it'. So I dug the hole, and when I thought it was three feet deep I sang out to him, and he came and looked at it.

'Three feet deep, eh?'

'Looks like it to me.'

'I'll measure it.' He pulled out a ruler, got down in the dirt and measured that bloody hole.

'No good, only two foot ten inches, dig out a bit more.'

He was like that with everything.

Taylor refused to take your word for anything, but he wasn't what I'd call a growling boss and he never gave me a hiding, he was just a hard, mean man.

I remember one time when Taylor, old Coondi and I were out on the boundary fence. Coondi had to carry the waterbags and I had to count the corner posts and for each one put a stone in my pocket. Taylor had a compass, he was taking the angles of the posts and making a map of the fence.

You see, in those days when you took up land you could take up, say, forty miles in any one direction, but within that forty miles there could be three or four bends. Might be a big hill along that

Foulkes-Taylor, Ethel Creek, 1924. (Battye 67327P)

forty mile line, or a river, or an outcrop of rocks. This meant there could be bits of land you were paying for but not using, but it also meant that there could be land you could be using that you hadn't paid for, depending on how the boundary fence had been mapped out. If there was a big hill on the boundary line you could gain more by fencing it into your property.

Taylor was keen to use every inch of land possible, that's why he was mapping. He was checking to see if the previous owner, who'd put the fence up, had missed any bits that they could have fenced in.

Anyway, this particular day was stinking hot. We'd driven out in Taylor's car, but after that it was footleather. We walked fifteen miles down the boundary fence and then fifteen miles back again. Taylor was cross about the fence. He said, 'This whole bloody fence is crooked and not to my advantage. Lord Nelson must have had the contract, or someone with one eye and one arsehole!'

When we got back to the car we boiled the billy and had a smoko. Coondi and I were exhausted by then, but Taylor was still full of energy. We climbed into the car and headed back towards the homestead.

I was that buggered I fell asleep in the back seat, but suddenly there was BANG! BANG! I woke up real quick and what did I see? Bloody Taylor shooting roos from the car. As long as there was daylight, he had to be doing something. He shot roos all the way back, we ended up with them roped on the trailer and hanging off the mudguards. In those days cars had large mudguards and you often stacked things on them.

The roos were for us blackfellas, that was our main diet, roos, damper and bread. It wasn't often we got a bit of sheep.

When people threw away crusts that were no good Taylor would come round and collect even the tiny, little bits to feed the chooks with. He reckoned it saved him money.

When you were out bush with Taylor he'd mix it up with you, have the same tucker and everything, but back at the homestead it was different. We ate at a table on the verandah, he ate in the dining-room.

I think the other reason we all found him hard to get on with was because he didn't have much of a sense of humour. We used to laugh about him of course, but I don't think he laughed much about us. I can't speak about what he was like in white society, he might have been different.

I'll never forget the time Old Pompee was yarding the sheep. They were running off in all directions and he just didn't seem to be able to bring them in. Taylor lost his temper.

'Give him a hand', he called to me 'Bloody bastard can't get them in!'

After a while he got sick of watching us both run around after the sheep and walked off, that was when Old Pompee started leaping up and down, in and out the sheep shouting, 'You bloody the Taylor bastard, you Taylor the bloody bastard!' On and on he went, doin' silly little dances and singin' out. I laughed and laughed, he was really funny.

Around this time my old playmate from Mt Edgar, Alma Corboy, got married to Charles Kingsford-Smith, who became famous later on for all that flying business. At that time he was jackerooing and seemed a nice enough bloke. Alma wanted me to go into the Bar for her wedding. I went in and saw them get married, I was real happy for her. That was the last time I saw Alma until the

Musterers, Corunna Downs Station, 1924. (Battye 67301P)

1940s, but I worked with her brother Des a bit.

Around 1924 a big cyclone came through the north. It came from the north-east with no warning and lasted three to four hours. There were no wirelesses around then, only telephones. I don't know if anyone had rung a warning through to Taylor or not, if they had he didn't tell us.

I was horseboy then. About daylight I got up and went to the stable, it was drizzling rain and there was a sharp wind that cut you like a knife, but it wasn't enough to stop working. I saddled my horse, but even then the wind was getting stronger and stronger. I gave up trying to ride him in the end, unsaddled him, and let him go out in the open. By that stage I had a feeling a cyclone might be on, and I thought he'd be safer out there.

I looked around and saw Tommy Stream, who wasn't much more than a kid then, blowin' away across the flats. He'd been trying to get to the kitchen. I rushed over and got him, but by Jeez, it was a battle to get him to the kitchen, the wind was getting very powerful and echoing all around us.

When the cyclone finally blew out we went to check the damage. Spinifex bushes had been blown all over the place and the leaves and smaller limbs had been stripped from the trees. The storeroom had completely lifted off its frame and all the flour and food in there had been spoiled. Eight date palms were knocked over and lying on the ground.

We went down to the One Mile and saw Emu Creek running bank to bank, and past that in some places, the windmill there was gone. Of the fifty-two windmills on Corunna, thirty-four of them were finished. The fences were all washed down and a lot of smaller creeks that had filled up with sand over the years were now gouged out. It was a miracle no stock was lost.

We worked flat out for the next few months repairing the damage. We started in the morning as soon as we could see and we never finished until we couldn't see. It made me realise that a cyclone is not a thing to be played with.

That same year I got word that Jack Doherty had been sent to Moore River Settlement to have treatment for his eyes. I knew Aunty would want him to get help with his eyes, but I think she also worried he might not come back. A lot of people that were taken away in those days never came back.

It was also around that time that the Afghan camel teams started to disappear from the Marble Bar area. Trucks were beginning to come in then and were putting the camel teams out of business. The Afghans moved further north into the Kimberley. I was sorry to see them go, they were wonderful people.

The Aboriginal mob on Corunna were marvellous. My cousin Maudie was there, she was a housegirl along with Wanggayingu, or Lily as we called her. Then there was Big Eadie, Alec, Nipper, Pompee, Jim Walters, Lucy, Rosie and so on.

Big Eadie was a ngayarda banujutha, he was Wanggayingu's man, and did mainly stockwork. There were twenty-two thousand sheep on Corunna then and it took at least a fortnight to shear them. My boss was Wanggayingu's brother, Albert Brockman, and when I was with him we concentrated mainly on the windmills. Albert nearly worked me to death, I think he enjoyed giving us young fellas a run for our money.

My cousin, Maudie, ended up staying on Corunna most of her life. She never left until 1950 when she went to the Onslow area and died around 1955. She was very good to me, she used to do a lot of my talking with the girls. Those Corunna women were

Corunna Downs Station, 1924. (Battye 67322P)

wonderful. They liked men, if you understand what I mean. They were very good. There were some very energetic women on Corunna then.

The corroborees there were wonderful too. We had them once a month. We would dance all night sometimes. There were some very good singers there amongst the women. Every corroboree we had was different and lasted a different length of time. Sometimes someone would make up a song and we'd all take a liking to it, we'd sing it over and over every night and still not get sick of it. We could make a good song last for weeks. Other times we'd get a song and teach it to others who didn't know it. Then they would go and teach it to another group and so on.

Some corroborees have what's called a Big dance in it. That's a special dance the women aren't allowed to see. Some dances they are allowed to see, but not the Big one. That's just for men.

Corroboree time is a very busy time. There's meat to be gotten, arrangements to be made, headdresses to be constructed, dances

Aboriginal group, Corunna Downs Station, 1924. (Battye 67302P)

to be worked out and songs to be learnt. It's very exciting. Depending
on what dances are going to be on, you might have to make three
or four different headdresses, and that takes time because some
of them are quite complicated and they all have to be painted
and decorated in the correct way. We used to make all our own
paint and help decorate one another. It all takes time and it all
has to be done properly, according to what the Law says. I used
to join in all the dances and songs. I loved that time. You wouldn't
recognise me now if I was dressed up like that.

I can't really explain to you how important those times were
to me. To sing and dance, to hear the women's voices singing out
high above the rest, it just made me feel good inside. I suppose
to people listening, our songs all sound the same, but to us they
are all different. Some were just for singing, some for dancing. They
were all entirely different to us.

The people there were wonderful storytellers too. At night we'd
sit around the campfire and the few old ones would tell us
Dreamtime stories. Can you imagine how it was for me then? The
fire, my friends, the moon and stars and us young blokes with
our mouths hanging open believing every word they said. Some
of those old people had a way of talking that sent shivers down

your spine. I can remember two stories from that time, I'll tell them to you.

The first one is about Gajiwarrgarda, a big snake who lived in the Dreamtime. He lived in a place called Mud Springs, it's on Bamboo Springs Station. For as long as that snake lived, there was water in that spring, but one day someone disturbed him and Gajiwarrgarda decided to leave. He came out and went west, as he travelled he left two ridges of rock on either side of him, he travelled for miles and miles until finally he got up onto the tablelands where he reared up and turned into a big rock. You can still see him standing there today and you can drive on the road that Gajiwarrgarda made, it's flat and level. The only thing is, if you go to his spring, it's dry on top now, you can't see any water there. Only one man used to be able to get water from there because that spring belonged to him, but he's dead now.

The second story is about Nyinggaranya, a giant. The old people really loved this one.

Nyinggaranya was so tall that when he laid down he was twelve miles long from head to toe. You can imagine that being so big he had an enormous appetite. One day he was out walking and saw a big mob of blackfellas camped near a pool. The people saw him coming and were terrified. They tried to run away but Nyinggaranya had magical powers. He just looked at them and they fell down dead. He went around and picked them all up by their legs and dashed their heads on the ground to make sure they were dead. Then he tucked them into the hair-belts he wore around his waist and arms.

Nyinggaranya dug a big hole about one hundred and fifty yards long near a pool. He looked around for some stones to tuck inside the people's bellies so they would cook quicker in the ground, but there were none. He walked off and got some from another place then came back and cooked them all in the big pit he'd dug.

When they were ready he pulled them out one by one, took the rocks out of their stomachs and ate the flesh. Slowly, all the rocks piled up one on top of the other and formed the Black Range that still runs through Hillside Station today. Now when the people walk past there they say quietly, 'Nyinggaranya left that there'.

Yes, they were great ones for talking that mob. They liked to go over things that had happened in the past. They weren't just concerned with Dreamtime stories, they used to talk about the days when old Drake-Brockman was there and they'd talk about the kids that had been taken away and so on. There was one travelling inspector from the Aborigines Department who used to go round there and they all agreed he was no good. Inspector Mitchell was his name. Instead of checking to see if the blackfellas were all right or had any complaints he would spend his time with the squatters and the managers drinking whisky.

One time, when someone was pretty sick, one of his relatives went to Mitchell and said, 'Come and look at my cousin, he's real sick, needs help'.

'Oh yes', said the inspector, 'well if he's still sick when I come again next year I'll have a look at him then'.

I think the other reason no one liked him was because he had been responsible for taking a lot of kids away.

Just talking about these old times makes me feel sad. When I think of it now, they were all good people. The dancing, the singing, the stories, my mates, all the things I used to live and work for, they're all gone. They were good old days then. Of course we were crook on the boss and the bloody tucker, but we were happy with each other, if you know what I mean.

There were many times during those years when I used to get really homesick for my aunties. I explained this to Taylor but he was never keen on letting me go off for a break to see them. He'd always tell me there was too much work to do and make me feel obligated to stay.

Anyway, for some reason I took sick all of a sudden, it was bladder trouble. Taylor tried to fix me himself, he had some of Dr Gillespie's old medical instruments, but he didn't know how to use them properly.

Dr Gillespie owned a neighbouring station and had visited Corunna often when the Drake-Brockmans ran it.

Eventually Taylor took me into the Marble Bar Hospital. I was one of his best workers so I suppose he wanted me fixed up quick.

It was illegal for people like me to be in a white hospital in those days, but some places were easier than others and I think because Taylor brought me in they thought it was all right. The

78

matron gave me the once over and then told me the doctor was coming up by train on Wednesday and would see me then. Taylor left me and went back to Corunna.

After a couple of days the matron said, 'No use you sitting here bored Jack, why don't you go down and visit your aunties. You can come back on Wednesday and see the doctor.'

That suited me just fine, so off I went. Aunty Dinah was real pleased to see me. She complained that her son Jack Doherty was still at Moore River. I think she was worrying about him.

I'd been with my family a few days down the reserve when the policeman sent his tracker down with a message that he wanted to see me straight away. I went to the station and he said, 'What are you doing in Marble Bar?'

'Waiting to see the doctor', I told him. 'Mr Taylor left me at the hospital and Matron said it was all right for me to stay with my family and to come up and see the doctor on Wednesday. Then I'm going back to Corunna.'

'I think you're just bludging, you blackfellas are all alike. You see that doctor quick smart and then get going, I don't want any bludgers round here. Just remember, I'll be keeping an eye on you!'

That man had his finger on all the Aboriginal people all the time. The white population around the Bar had decreased by then so he was the only policeman stationed there.

I saw the doctor on Wednesday and he gave me some medicine that seemed to help, but it didn't completely cure me because I was to suffer from that same complaint on and off for the rest of my life.

I said goodbye to Aunty, she wanted me to stay longer but I thought I would get in trouble with the policeman if I did, so it was best to leave. I've been like that all my life, tried to avoid trouble, tried to do the right thing. I'm a quiet-living sort of person but if I think something's right, I generally stick to it.

When I returned to Corunna Joe Exton told me that Foulkes-Taylor had gone to Perth for a holiday. I told him about the way the policeman had carried on in the Bar, but he didn't think it was important. With Taylor away, I thought it was a good opportunity to leave. My cousin, Clancy Doherty, had been on Corunna working for a few months and he was keen to leave too,

Carting wool bales, Corunna Downs Station, date unknown. (Battye 67355P)

so we decided to walk back over to Limestone and see if there was any work there.

The others on Corunna didn't want me to leave, especially Wanggayingu, she wanted me to stay. We were all very fond of one another by then. As we were walking off Wanggayingu ran after me and took the plaited leather belt from around her waist and gave it to me as a gift. She'd bought the belt from Jack Stanton, who made a lot of plaited belts and hatbands from leather. I'd always admired it.

Jack used to work round all the stations. He was very good with his hands and the leather goods he made were very popular.

'Thank you', I said, 'that's very nice of you'.

'You come back Jack, don't stay away too long, we're all one family here.'

I was sad to go, to leave my friends and relations, but I knew if I waited till Taylor got back from Perth I might never get away, and I didn't want to have to work under hard conditions all my life. I wanted something better, if I couldn't find it then I might go back, but at least I was going to try.

When Tommy Mallett, the owner, spotted me on Limestone he said, 'Good to see you Jack, I'm shorthanded at present, I can do with an extra man, but I'm surprised Taylor has let you go.

'He's in Perth', I told him. Tommy had asked Taylor before if I could go and work for him, to help out when they were shorthanded and so on, but Taylor had always refused to lend me to anyone. I think he was worried I might not come back.

When Taylor came back from his holiday he came out to Limestone and asked for me back, but Tommy said, 'He's out on the run at present, so I can't ask him, but as for me, I don't want to let him go. I want him to stay here, he's a good worker.'

'That's why I want him back.'

'Well you can't have him.'

'You tell him if he ever wants a job there's one waiting for him', said Taylor and left.

Everyone told me that night that Taylor and Tommy had exchanged words over me. If I had've chosen to, I could have returned to Corunna, Tommy would have let me go. It was a hard decision. To tell you the truth, I was torn between the two for different reasons. On Limestone conditions were good, the boss was good, the food was good, but it wasn't any good as far as women were concerned. My stomach was happy on Limestone, but my heart was at Corunna.

In the end the working conditions and hope for a better future won through. It turned out to be a wise decision because over the next few years all my mates left Corunna one by one. That was hard for them because it was part of their tribal area and some of them had very deep feelings for the place, but in the end they were the same as me, they just got fed up with the working conditions. You see, you can't expect people to give their guts away for nothing. You can't work them and work them, not feed them properly, and expect them to stay. I think they all decided they wanted something better too.

7

Making My Own Way
1927-1931

I stayed on Limestone for six months until the work ran out. That was the trouble with station work, it was seasonal. Every summer we were stood down, but then expected to turn up when they needed us again. It wasn't satisfactory at all.

I decided to go pink-eye to Yarrie Station because there were meetings on there and some young fellas were being put through the Law. I hitched a lift out in a truck. A month later, after all the dancing and singing were over, I came in with my mates Jenkins and Irishman Jack, to the Moolyella area. We panned for tin around there, trying to fill in time until the stations wanted labour again.

We were all sitting playing cards one day when a bloke called Arthur Meehan turned up. He was one of the sons of John Patrick Meehan.

'Any of you fellas want a job?' he asked.

'I do', I said.

'You done station work before?'

'Too right!'

'You're hired. I've got some horses waiting to be picked up on Limestone. You can come with me now and help me get them down to Austin Downs Station at Cue.' I left my friends and went back to Limestone.

But when Tommy Mallett, the owner of Limestone Station, heard that I'd accepted a job he said, 'Why don't you stay around here Jack, there'll be work sooner or later and this is your area. I don't like to lose a good man.'

82

I was tempted, but I was also feeling adventurous. I wanted to get out of my own area for a while. I thought the job with Arthur Meehan might lead to something else, it was worth a try anyway.

What surprised me most about Austin Downs was the lack of Aboriginal people. There was only Jack O'Brien and his missus, Huey King and Rita, Moppy, Aubrey, Jupiter and me.

Jupiter was about sixty-years old, a ngayarda banujutha, and a good old fella. We got on well. He'd been there for years. Jack O'Brien was a ngayarda banujutha too, but he was only there when there was shearing to be done. Huey and Rita were mardamardas and they looked after the outcamp. That left Moppy and Aubrey, who were also mardamardas, and me, to do the stockwork. There were about thirty-five thousand head of sheep on the station then and five hundred head of cattle so we were kept pretty busy.

Later Meehan got in Minnie Ugle to cook. He sang out to me one day, 'Got a woman for you now Jack, the new cook!'

I took one look and said, 'You can have that one, she's too wrinkly for me!'

Minnie only ended up staying two weeks. They had trouble keeping cooks and yardmen because of Mother Meehan, she liked to interfere whenever she could. No one could get on with her, black or white. I remember after Minnie left there were a couple of cooks supposed to be coming out, but they spent a day in the pub at Cue, heard all about Mother Meehan, and turned round and went back to Perth! That happened a number of times. She didn't affect me too much because I didn't have to have a lot to do with her, however, the ones that did used to complain all the time.

I didn't get on with Mother Meehan's roo dog. He'd been given to her by a publican and was called Roger. He had his own kennel and was tied to it during the day. I'd been nervous of roo dogs ever since one had bitten me on the head as a kid and I think Roger sensed this. He realised he had some kind of power over me because he learnt to recognise my footsteps. Whenever he heard me coming he'd leap out barking loudly and dragging his kennel behind him trying to get me.

Apart from Roger and his mistress, Arthur Meehan and all the other Meehan men were real good blokes. They always gave swagmen coming through a feed, even if Mother objected, and they were very good to work for.

Through mixing with the few Aboriginal people in the area I soon discovered that it wasn't only Austin Downs that didn't have many Mulbas, it was the same all around the Murchison. I was told they'd all been taken away by the police and sent to government settlements and missions by order of the Aborigines Department. The idea was to take people, especially kids, away from their families and tribal area and to bring them up as white people. It seemed silly to me, but then the governments had a lot of silly ideas when it came to blackfellas.

The pay on Austin Downs was good, the tucker was good, and black and white ate together so that was good too. While I was there Meehan bought Mt Vernon Station, so I found myself working between the two, mustering sheep and cattle. Mt Vernon was a good place to work, but a bit isolated, I didn't get to see many of my own people when I was there. Sometimes a few of us would sit round the campfire and sing songs, but we usually liked to wait until there was a muster on because with more people it made it more worthwhile. They weren't real proper corroborees, not like the ones I was used to, but I suppose they were better than nothing.

I saved all my pay while I was working for Meehans and went into Meekatharra one day and bought a gramophone from the shop there. I thought it'd be nice to be able to turn on a bit of music whenever I liked instead of having to wait for the mustering to start before I could hear a bit of good singing. It was whiteman's music, but I was interested in that too.

After I'd had the gramophone a few months I met up with a bloke who had a BSA motorbike. He saw my gramophone and suggested we swap because he didn't need his bike anymore. I was sick of playing it by then and I'd never had a bike, so I agreed. I thought now I owned a motorbike I'd better do the right thing and get a licence so I went and saw the two policemen there, Sergeant Bill Fennings, who was nicknamed Bramby Mick, and Barney Rule. They were both good fellas.

'It's not really necessary to have a licence for a bike', they told me, 'but seeing as how you're interested we'll give you one anyway'.

I didn't have to sit for a test or anything, they just filled out a form in a little book they had.

Now and then, when I was having a break from the station, I'd go into the races at Meeka and Cue. Race time was always a big event and attracted people from all round the area, so it was the best opportunity I had of mixing with other Aboriginal people. I was very good at saving my money, but at race time I indulged myself by booking into the Royal Mail Hotel in Meekatharra.

The first time I stayed there I met a woman called Topsy, who was working at Greenwood Station. She used to see me sitting on the steps of the hotel in my suit. She'd walk past and smile and wave. Pretty soon we went from waving to talking. She was very easy to talk to and we got on well together. I took her to the pictures and whatever else was on in town. I loved the pictures and so did she. I remember the first silent movie I ever saw was on Jack Dempsey, the boxer, and I thought it was wonderful. There's nothing I like more than seeing a good fight. Later on, Gracie Fields and Bob Hope became two of my favorites. A lot of my mates liked cowboy films but I didn't take to them, they had too much pretend in them. All that shooting and the gun never runs out of bullets. How can you kill fifty Indians with a gun that only holds six cartridges? And those horses! Galloping, galloping, like bloody motorcars, never running out of steam! I used to laugh in those bits because I knew there was as much truth in them as was in Charlie Alcorn's stories.

Anyhow, it wasn't long before Topsy and me were sweethearts. I didn't want to leave her behind when it was time for me to return to station work, so I left her temporarily with Mrs Meegan, the storekeeper's wife in Daydawn. Then I went out to Austin Downs to talk to the boss and fix things up so that she could come out with me. When I came back to get her at the end of the day she was gone.

'A man came and took her away', Mrs Meegan told me. I went and saw the police but they said there was nothing they could do about it. You see, tribally she belonged to the ngayarda banujutha who had come in and forced her to leave. She'd been wanting to get away from him because he was cruel to her, he used to beat

Jack McPhee on the steps of a hotel, Meekatharra, Christmas 1928.

her something awful. That's why I was worried, I knew what she was going back to. In the end I accepted that I just had to leave it. So, that was the end of my first real romance.

Towards the end of 1928 my old mate Billy Moses turned up on his Red Indian bike. He had been working around the area and was on his way back to the Bar. He, Matt Narrier, who was another mardamarda, and I all decided we'd book into the Royal Mail and treat ourselves to a real good Christmas. That's what we did. Bill didn't have much money, so I paid for him, he never had any decent clothes either, so while we were there he used to wear my spare suit.

We stayed together for two weeks and really enjoyed ourselves. At the end of that time Bill headed off on his bike for the Bar. I heard later that it gave him so much trouble he ended up ditching it in the bush and hitching a lift with a truck.

He'd wanted me to go home with him. 'You belong there', he told me.

And it was true, I did. But I was wanting something better, and at that point in my life, I was about twenty-three, I felt I was starting to get it. I had a good job, clothes, money in my pocket, and I was learning to read and write as well. The whiteman I was sharing a room with on Austin Downs, Bill Munn, was helping me.

After work I'd ask him to write different words, and he'd put them down on paper and I'd copy them. I learnt how to spell short words first, then I went on to bigger ones. Bill used to write letters for me to Jack Doherty at Moore River Settlement. It was a good thing that I learnt to read and write because if you don't other people can always get the better of you. Also, it meant that later on I could write to the Aborigines Department and tell them just what I thought of them.

In 1929 I sold my bike to Huey King, I had my eye on a Chev Tourer, a car that a bloke owned in Cue. It was nearly brand new and I'd heard he wanted to sell it. I worked on Austin Downs for a few months longer saving everything I could so I could buy the Chev.

One day the boss came to me and said, 'Depression's really starting to hit us Jack. Things are going to be very, very tough here. I'm sorry, but I'll have to either cut you off altogether or reduce your pay.'

I wasn't sure what to do, I thought about it for a while and then said, 'What about letting me go roo shooting? I'll stay in the area so I can give you a hand when you need it, and it'll be good money for me because their price is up at the moment.' He thought that was a good idea and we agreed to keep in touch.

I left Austin Downs then and went into Cue and bought the Chev for one hundred and twenty quid, I was very pleased with it because it had only done one hundred and fifty miles. Then I bought a thirty-two calibre rifle, some ammo and enough supplies to last me a few weeks.

While I was in Cue I met up with a white bloke who was out of work and decided he was interested in coming shooting with me. He reckoned he'd pull his weight and he seemed all right, so I agreed. I don't think he realised then what hard work it was, because as soon as we sold our first lot of skins he went on a binge and that was the last I ever saw of him.

Roo shooting is a terribly hard job for one man. It's best to limit your shoot to only thirty or forty a night. Some nights I was bloody silly and shot up to fifty, that made it damn hard to get everything done the following day. I only did that a couple of nights and then decided I was a mad bugger, and stuck to the thirty a night.

There's no set time for how long it will take you to shoot thirty roos. It might take a few hours, it might take all night, it all depends on how many come in to drink.

My routine was this. Every afternoon, around five or five-thirty, I'd go down to the waterhole and check that the little hiding place I'd made myself was still all right. Roos aren't stupid, if they see you standing there with a rifle they're not going to come in. I'd camp in that cubby and wait until they came in, then when they'd settled down I'd start shooting. When that lot took off I'd have to wait until another lot came in, and so on, until I'd had my kill. Most nights I'd knock off anywhere between ten pm and two am.

If I wasn't too tired I'd start to skin them straight away, it's easier then because their bodies are still soft and you can get quite

Skinning a kangaroo, date and place unknown. (Battye 7348596)

a few done quickly. If you leave them till morning, it's much harder work.

Once the skinning was finished I'd cart the carcasses at least half a mile away to where there was plenty of wood so I could burn them when they'd dried out a bit. If you leave the carcasses near the waterhole the roos won't come in because they can smell death.

Each skin has to be pegged and painted with arsenic to get rid of the bugs. Takes about a day and a night for the skin to dry out properly. Once they were dry I'd pull them off the pegs, trim them, paint them with arsenic again and stack them.

It's a hard life, and by the time the afternoon comes round you're tired and hungry and wonder if it's worth it all. I'd cook a bit of tucker for myself then, that always cheered me up, and then I'd try and get some sleep, so I wouldn't be too tired to shoot again that night.

On the average I was getting two hundred skins a week and being paid about thirteen pounds a hundred. It was damn good money for those days.

Jobs were very scarce during the Depression and white people as well as black were very, very poor. I remember there were four hundred white people camped between Cue and Meekatharra around that time. They were working on a government project building a dam. The men had to work two weeks on and two weeks off, so it gave each family a chance to earn a little bit of money. There were other men going from station to station begging for food and work. Some of them had no boots because their shoes had worn out through walking so far and they couldn't afford to replace them. I remember women walking with one canvas shoe and one leather shoe, and with their toenails poking through where their shoes had worn out. It was a very hard time.

After I'd been out bush a few weeks I'd give myself a break by going into Meeka for a few days and spoiling myself. I made sure I ate well and relaxed a little. I'd buy myself tinned fruit, which I loved, and bacon, which was cheap in those days.

It was during this time that I palled up with Florrie. She lived in Nannine and was married to a whitefella, she had a child too. He used to neglect them and I think she was very lonely. Anyway, when she knew I was in Meeka she'd come in and see me. She was a mardamarda like me. I'd take her back to her place in the Chev and stay a few days, her husband was never there. I think he only came when it suited him, and that wasn't very often. Florrie and I got on well together and it gave me something to look forward to after being out bush for weeks on my own.

I continued to shoot roos for about eight months and over this time Florrie and I began to get serious. I thought that if we were going to stay like that I would need a proper job because roo shooting was too hard a life for a woman and kid.

In 1930 Meehan asked me if I would come back to Austin Downs and give them a hand with a droving trip. We mustered up some bullocks and took them into Cue. I stayed on Austin Downs for a few more months but then the work ran out again, so Meehan asked around and found a job for me on Mt Seabrook Station. I decided to take it even though the pay wasn't much because I was looking for the kind of job that would be all right if you had a woman with you. I decided to sell the Chev before I went to Mt Seabrook because I'd broken the front axle on my last trip out bush and hadn't been able to repair it. I sold it for eighty quid to a bloke who reckoned he could fix it up. I told Florrie about the Mt Seabrook job and said that when I was going all right I'd send for her.

I soon realised that the pay I was getting wasn't enough to keep two people, so I decided that I would need to scrape around for extra work if I was going to take Florrie on. It turned out that wasn't necessary because while I was on Mt Seabrook I found out that another fella had been courting Florrie while I was away and had cut me out completely.

I seemed to have had real bad luck with women at that time in my life. I thought it might be a good idea not to get involved with anymore who had complications in their lives. Next time I took up with a woman, I was going to make sure that there wasn't another fella hiding in the bushes waiting for his turn.

I was sent away from the homestead on Mt Seabrook to look after the windmills and to check some of the fencing at the outcamp. After a few months a couple called Willie and Alice were sent out there too. We all had to do the same kind of work, checking fences, riding horses all day, mustering and so on. I quite enjoyed working on Mt Seabrook and would have stayed there longer except for the argument that I had with Nick Campbell, the manager.

It wasn't Nick's fault, it was Willie's. Somehow he got it into his head that I was fooling around with Alice, and he went and complained to Nick and asked him to do something. Nick called me in, told me what Willie had said, and asked, 'What are you going to do about it Jack?'

'I'm not going round with her, we're talking a bit, can I help it if she likes my company?'

'Willie's very upset.'

'Might be better if I leave then.' I was a silly bugger, I'd been through the same thing twice before, and now here I was doing it again. I thought I'd better get while the going was good.

'There should be a stone truck coming through soon', Nick said. 'It goes out to Charlie Livingstone's Show and to Peak Hill, I'll arrange for you to get a lift on that.'

It was three weeks before the truck came through. I said goodbye to Willie and Alice. Alice was sorry to see me go but it was no use me staying there and having us fighting each other all the time.

I got dropped off at Charlie Livingstone's Show, and he needed a bloke to give him a hand for a while.

I'd been there a few weeks when I thought it might be a good idea to try and get my Miner's Rights. That way instead of working for Charlie I could work for myself. I went into Meeka and enquired about Miner's Rights but they told me that I couldn't have it.

'Why?' I asked.

'Because it's illegal', they told me.

'Why's that?'

'Because you're a native, only whitemen are allowed Miner's Rights.'

That was news to me, I didn't see why we couldn't all have Miner's Rights. It didn't seem fair. There was no use arguing about it, I wasn't the kind of bloke that made trouble. I just accepted that that was that, and went back to Charlie's Show.

Anyway, much to my surprise, it wasn't long before a letter turned up for me from Jack Doherty. I hadn't heard from him for a while.

He was still in Moore River Native Settlement and was sick and he wanted me to go and visit him. He said my old Uncle Hector was in the Settlement too and very ill. That made me really keen to go because I hadn't seen either of them for years and they were both close to me. Uncle Hector was the one who used to sit me on his knee and sing corroboree songs. I had very fond memories of him and I was determined to see them both. I showed Charlie my letter and told him I had to go. He said if he got something out of the crushing later on he would send it on.

I packed up my swag and hitched a lift into Meekatharra where I sent a wire to Jack telling him I was coming. Then I caught a train.

You know, I think that bloody train must have pulled in at every place it could think of before we finally hit Mogumber Siding, which was about eight miles from the Settlement. I grabbed my swag and jumped off the train and onto the platform. I was wondering what Moore River would be like.

8

Moore River Settlement
1931-1932

It was just daylight and to my surprise there was a group of people standing there. A man walked over and said, 'You Jack McPhee?'

'Yes.'

'What have you come for?'

'My cousin's sick at the Settlement, I want to visit him.'

'That's a pretty good excuse isn't it?'

I didn't know what to say to that. Who was this fella talking to me anyway?

'Would you know your cousin if you saw him?'

'Yes.'

He called a bloke forward from down behind him in the dark and said, 'Who's this then?'

'That's my cousin, Jack Doherty.'

'So you really do know him. All right, you can go out to the Settlement, but you better mind yourself. You never got my permission to come here, I could gaol you if I wanted to, you know.'

We walked with a man called Mr Hedge to a truck. As we were driving away he said, 'Don't take any notice of that bastard. I don't like him either and I'm a whiteman.'

It turned out that bloke was A.O. Neville himself, the Chief Protector of Aborigines. I don't know how he got that job because I don't think he liked Aboriginal people. And he didn't seem to like me in particular, a strange Aboriginal person, coming to the Settlement without his permission. I was to learn the hard way over the years that followed that he didn't like blackfellas having

Moore River Settlement with church at centre, date unknown. (Battye BA 368/4)

initiative of their own.

It was about six to eight miles through sandplain country before you got to the Settlement. You wouldn't have known it was there. Looking back now, I think that's what the government wanted. We weren't considered of use to anybody, except for cheap labour, so those of us that didn't belong in that category were nothing but a problem. They wanted to keep us out of sight.

When we reached Moore River, Jack had to take me straight into the office to see Arthur Neal, the Superintendent. He was a big man with a handlebar moustache.

'Why are you here?', he asked when Jack introduced me.

'I come to see this bloke', I pointed to Jack.

'You're not allowed to take women away from here.'

'I didn't come to do that.' To tell you the truth, I was a bit sick of women by then. I'd decided to leave them alone for a while.

'Are you going to work or pay for your board?'

'Well, I'd like a week's holiday and then I'll do whatever work

Children, Moore River Settlement. (Battye 4965B/29)

you want.'

'Hmmn, do you have any money on you?'

'Yes.'

'Right, you hand it over now. No money is allowed in the camp where you'll be staying. If you want to buy something at the store you can come and get your money when you need it.' He held out his hand and I passed my money over. 'After your holiday you can go out on the wagon collecting firewood with the boys.' I agreed to that and we left the office.

When outside I looked at Jack. I was beginning to wonder what kind of place this was.

'Come and see Uncle Hector before we talk', he said.

Hector was in his seventies by then and dying. He'd been sent to Moore River for medical treatment, but they hadn't been able to do anything for him. When I saw him he was unconscious and nearly dead. Sister Newman, the Church of England missionary there, arranged his funeral a few days later. I was very upset because Hector was very close to Jack and me.

Jack showed me around Moore River and as we went we talked.

Moore River Settlement showing the 'Boob', small white shed on the right. (Royal Western Australian Historical Society, Battye 5986B)

'This part is called the compound', he told me, 'there's the church, sewing room, dormitories where they keep all the kids, store, you've seen the office and the hospital'.

'Whose kids are they?'

'Anybody's. Some got their names changed. You know whitefellas if they can't get their tongue around your name they call you something else. No one be able to find these kids now.'

I was thinking to myself, to take a child from its mother is a cruel thing. The mother has given the life, suffered for it, it's not right that life is taken from her.

'When a family comes in', said Jack, 'the kids live in dormitories, others down in the camp'.

We walked on a bit further and Jack said, 'You watch out for the boob brother'. He pointed to a small, galvanised iron building off in the distance.

'What's that?'

'Gaol! Don't take much to get in there.'

'What gets you in there?'

'Messin' with women, bein' cheeky, anything. Kids in there

sometimes. Better you stay on the boss's good side. He's got all the say.'

'Jeez Jack, is this a prison?'

He laughed. 'Trackers here too. Bring you back if you run away.'

'Can't you do something?'

'Who will listen brother? Boss reads all the mail that goes out and comes in.'

'You mean he read all those letters I sent you?'

'Yeah.'

'No wonder he ask me about woman!'

'Good to see you anyway brother', Jack laughed. 'We got some nice womans here.'

'Ooh no, ooh no, I'm giving that one a break for a while! Tell me about tucker, that's better than woman.'

'Bread and fat in the morning, watery stew or soup at lunch, bread and treacle for dinner. No milk or sugar in your tea. If there's meat going, the ration is one chop, one man. The only time we get extra is if Billy Warrell, who's camped over there in those sandhills, sends roo in.'

'Can't live on that.'

'Unless you want to use your money to buy from the store, you won't have any choice. Some of the girls who've been out working do that.'

'Maybe I better pal up with one of them! Just friends, you know.'

'Helen Bunda's here.'

'Yeah?!'

'She wants to go out to work but they won't let her. Neville wants her to go back to Brockmans', but she won't go.'

'Why not?'

'Dunno.'

'She got a man?'

'Yeah, brother.'

'I better forget about her then, I have no luck with those ones! Where's your camp Jack?'

'Not here, brother, down there.' He pointed to some old huts a long way off. 'It's not much', he said, 'but it's all there is'.

As we headed towards the camp Jack told me that he worked as an orderly in the hospital, so he'd been able to spend quite

Moore River Settlement, 1920s. (Battye BA 368/4)

a bit of time with Hector, who had been there over a year.

Jack said they hadn't been able to do anything about his eyes. He'd been sent out to work at different places but they always sent him back because they wanted a bloke who could see good. It was a pity, because Jack was a very strong, powerful man, as strong as Clancy McKenna. He could've done all sorts of work if it hadn't been for his eyes.

'You saved much money?', I asked him.

'Could have saved more if they'd given all me pay. Bloody Aborigines Department gets more than I do.'

'Why?'

'Dunno.'

'Can you get it back?'

'You got to have a good reason. The ones that can't write, kiss it goodbye.'

'What happens to it then?'

'I've heard it goes to looking after us.' Jack looked at me and we both laughed.

When we got back to the camp Jack introduced me to his wife Jean. She was from the Goldfields and very light in colour, but still a native according to the Aborigines Department. She had been brought up by the Salvation Army after they took her away from her mother and trained as a domestic. It seemed to me it was the same old story. Just enough education to make us useful to the whiteman but not enough to make us equal.

It was very rough in the camp. No proper houses, no sanitation.

Carting wood, Moore River Settlement. (Battye 368/4)

You made your own shelter from whatever you could scrounge in the bush. Some people had managed to make mud floors. Hessian bags were painted with whitewash for walls and tied into bush timber which was used to make a rough frame. You were lucky if you could find a bit of tin for a roof. The water in the river was a blackish colour so I wasn't keen to drink that. I got together with a few other men and we dug a soak, we had good water after that.

After my holiday I started work with Mr Hedge. I liked him because he was a gentleman and didn't carry on the way I soon found out the others did. When we were working he'd make you a cup of tea and treat you the same as himself. I think he had a woman there, but he stuck to her and didn't go chasing all the others. He was a good bloke.

Every day I would pick up the horses and get the team ready to go out and cut wood. Four or five of us went out at a time.

It was very easy work compared to what I was used to. When the wagon was full we returned to the Settlement and that was it for the day.

I found one of my biggest problems was boredom. There was nothing to do. No cattle to look after, no sheep to yard, no windmills to fix, no nothing. People were very bored. The women there seemed to be the most affected. They were very depressed. Some of them would just sit and stare. There was nothing for them, only gambling. They had no hope of leaving. A lot of them wanted to go back to their homeland, they were pining for it. It was very sad to see them like that.

I filled my time in by talking with the girls whenever I could. They were all interested in me because I was new and had lots of stories to tell. It's funny, but at first all the girls looked the same to me and I couldn't work out why. Then I realised it was their clothes, they all wore a sort of khaki denim. Even their underpants were made out of it, don't ask me how I know. The only ones that had anything nice were those who had been working and bought things from their pay. Girls who went out to work from Moore River only returned if their job finished or if they got pregnant, which was quite often.

I took up with one girl at the Settlement, but then another bloke cut me out so I decided to freelance for a while. I went from one to the other without getting really serious with any of them. You had to be careful with Neal because if he thought you were being a good boy he treated you good, but if you got on the wrong side of him it was a different story.

There were rules at the Settlement for everything, and I have to admit I found it very frustrating because I wasn't used to living in such a strict way. Funnily enough though, I soon found myself becoming just like everyone else, and accepting that I was living in a gaolhouse. It was the kind of place that stopped you from wanting to really better yourself.

While I was there Oscar Little, who had become a friend of mine, ran away with his girlfriend Maggie. Neal sent Kimberley, the black tracker, after them. He brought them back and they were put in the boob for a few days each. Not many people managed to escape from there and not get caught.

Matron with babies, Moore River Settlement. (Battye BA 368/4)

Now, getting back to women again, I used to feel sorry for some of them. They often talked about Neal and Larter, the bloke who was in charge of the laundry. There were eight women who worked in the laundry and they ranged in age from eighteen to about thirty. Larter was a rough man, grubby and mean and bad with the language. The girls used to say, 'He's after woman all the time!'

Women weren't safe with him. He had no respect. Even if the girls had boyfriends he'd still have a go.

Neal chased the women too, but he wasn't so obvious. His wife was the matron there and she was always sneaking around trying to catch him. Neal wasn't going to bother with her when he had all those young ones. When Matron went on her trips to Perth, Neal would have a field day. He could pick whatever girls he liked to do his cooking and cleaning. None of them wanted the job because it meant you got him too. He could punish you if you didn't go his way. I know he fathered a few kids but he never owned up to any.

There was a problem with marriages there too. In those days Aboriginal people weren't allowed to marry unless they had the official permission of the Aborigines Department. That meant you had to talk to Neal about it first, he was the first link in the chain. He'd say things like, 'Are you sure she's the right one for you?' and all that bulldust. Then, when it suited him, he'd send for your girl.

'So you want to marry so and so?'

'Yes.'

'Well, you'll have to have a long talk to me about it.' Then he'd take them into the storeroom where they kept the bags of flour and have them in there. I've seen girls coming out myself with flour all over their dresses. He was very shrewd that way because any kids that came along ended up with someone else's name, not his. He always pressured Neville to approve the marriages of the girls he slept with.

Those two men were as bad as the squatters in that respect. As for us blackfellas, we just accepted that that was the way of it. There was nothing we could do, and who were we going to complain to, Neal?!

I remember one night a message was sent down to the camp that Neal wanted to see me. You weren't allowed into the compound after dark unless you were sent for, though we often used to sneak back and forth.

When I went to the office Neal had a revolver in his hand and Larter was there with his shotgun. Neal said, 'You're a stranger here aren't you Jack? You haven't been here long compared with the others.'

'Not long', I replied as I kept an eye on his gun.

'Well, we're after two strangers tonight. They've been hanging around after dark. Not friends of yours are they Jack?'

'No.'

'Better not be! One bloke is big built, he might want a fight. I want you to help us bring them in. If they won't come in, we'll shoot them.'

I was sent off with Larter and I was praying we wouldn't see those blokes. Everyone knew who they were, we'd been giving them food at night because they had none. They had relatives in the compound they wanted to see, a daughter and a sister, I think. And of course since they'd been hanging around they'd picked up a couple of girlfriends as well, but they weren't doing any harm.

Luckily, we didn't see them that night, someone must have warned them. I was worried I might be forced to shoot and if it's one thing I couldn't do, it's kill another human being. I don't think Neal or Larter were so interested in catching those men as having a bit of sport. They thought they were kings.

Even though it was hard and rough at the Settlement, it wasn't all doom and gloom, because we all had each other and I made some very good friends there. Sister Newman used to put dances on sometimes on a Wednesday night, while she played the piano we all jigged around. It was new to me because I only knew the blackfella way of dancing. Johnson Morton, another mardamarda there, got his wife to teach me the whiteman's way. In those days they were very strong on telling you that the blackfella way was wrong and that none of us must go back to those ways. A lot of people took this seriously and gave up their language and everything. As for me, I suppose I was silly enough to think I could have the best of both worlds. I wanted what the blackman could give me and what the whiteman could give me. As my life turned out it was stupid of me to even consider that.

Church was on every Sunday and a lot of people went. I wasn't keen on it myself but Jack and Jean were very keen so I went along to please them and to be sociable. You see, Jack and I were very close and I just hated to disappoint him over anything. I learnt a few hymns there, which I still know, and I can recite the Lord's Prayer off by heart. Jack's favorite hymn was 'Jesus Keep Me Near the Cross'. Sometimes, when I'm thinking of him now, I sing that and it makes me cry.

Going to church soon led to Sister Newman and Jack wanting me to be baptised. I thought I could live without it myself, but Jack wanted me to go to heaven so I finally agreed. Sister Newman chose Oscar Little to tip the bottle of water over my head because he was my friend. That's how he came to be my godfather even though he's younger than me.

When people heard that I was going to be baptised they all decided to come to the service, it was embarrassing. The girls were the worst, giggling and carrying on. They knew I wasn't really interested in the baptism business and they made jokes like, 'You the biggest baby we ever seen done, Jack', or 'You got to be a good boy now, Jack'.

Helen Bunda came up to me and said, 'You belong to God now Jack', and all the girls laughed.

I liked Helen. She was a close relation to me and we often had little talks. I remember her saying, 'I've been here too long and too often Jack. I want to go home, back North. I don't want to go to Brockmans'. They work you to death and give you nothing.'

'I wish I could help you Helen', I said, 'but there's nothing I can do'.

'We're all the same here Jack, we're lost people.'

You'll have realised by now that despite my good intentions I couldn't stay away from the girls. I thought it was all right as long as I stuck to the freelancing, but somehow, before I knew it, I became serious with a girl called Susie Smith. She was from the Ashburton area, Prairie Downs Station, and her real name was Bessie Connaughton, but they changed her name when she was brought to the Settlement. Her Aboriginal name was Mularna, but no one called her by that.

Susie had been at Moore River since 1924. She had been sent

out to various places to work from the Settlement, sometimes to the country, but she had been unhappy in most of her jobs. She was only young and she got very lonely.

Also, Susie was a high-spirited girl, I think she used to get a bit cheeky sometimes, that was how she'd lost her last job. You see, in those days they expected a servant to do exactly as they were told, right or wrong, I think Susie got sick of that.

She told me she'd been sent to the Native and Half-Caste Girls Home in East Perth after her last job and she wanted to stay there and find her own work. Work that she was happy with. Neville wouldn't let her. He sent a warrant to the Commissioner of Police for Susie's removal back to Moore River. We were classed like criminals then. Susie hated the Settlement, it was the last place in the world she wanted to go.

Since she'd been back at Moore River she told me she'd written to Neville and asked him to find her another job. She'd threatened to run away if he didn't. Susie knew there was no point in running away because they'd only bring her back, it was just that she was very unhappy there.

Susie and I got on well. She was pretty, a good cook, had a sense of humour and was a hard worker. I think she liked me because she could see I was dependable and wanted to get on in the world. Everything was going along all right until Neal got wind of things. He called me up to his office one day and wanted to know what was going on.

'Well, we're seeing each other', I told him.

'Oh yes, well you better watch yourself. You have your own life to lead and I won't interfere as long as you behave, but I can't guarantee what kind of woman she is.' I decided to just ignore anything he said.

Pretty soon Jack, and Bob Allen, who was a tracker from the North, were telling me I should get married. They thought Susie and I were a good match, but their opinion was based on Susie coming from the North. You see, in Moore River at that time there were a lot of good women from the south of Western Australia, and I think they were worried I might take up with one of them and marry away from my own country. Northerners were very strong on that business, they liked you to stick to your own countrymen.

It was the same even amongst the kids.

I started to think about it, weighing everything up. I knew I'd have to settle down sooner or later and she was a good cook. Also, lots of stations liked to hire married couples, so it could make it easier for me to find a job. In the end I asked her to marry me and she agreed, it was October 1932 by then. I was about twenty-seven.

I went to the office to see Neal and he said, 'I don't know Jack, are you sure you're doing the right thing?'

'I think so.'

'You haven't got a job.'

'I'll get one.'

'I'll have to write to Neville for permission. I'll put you both on six months' probation from today, and at the end of that time, if you conduct yourself properly, it might be all right.'

Neal told me later that Neville had written to say he would see me on his next visit to Moore River. Neville came in December of that year and I was waiting for him to call me into the office, but he never did, he talked to Neal about me instead. That's what I could never work out, he was supposed to be our Protector but he wasn't interested in anything we had to say.

I found out there were some men leaving to work up North and I thought it could be a good opportunity for me, so I asked Neal if I could go, but he told me the quota was full. I decided to take things into my own hands and write to Billy Martin, who owned Mt Padbury Station. I thought he might be looking for a married couple and he knew my reputation as a hard worker. I took my letter to the office so Neal could read it. Fortunately he approved it and said he would send it off for me.

A reply came ten days later with money for the train fare. Neal called me up, showed me the letter and said he had written to Neville. In January 1933 he posted an official notice on the office door about our marriage. We were married in February by the Church of England minister.

Before we left Neal reminded me, 'Don't forget Jack, the Aborigines Department only gave you permission to marry Susie as long as you never take her to Prairie Downs Station. You go onto there, and you'll be in trouble.' Prairie Downs wasn't too far from Mt

Jack McPhee and Susie Smith, wedding day, Moore River Settlement, 1932. Jack Doherty is on the left.

Padbury but I wasn't going to argue. Getting married had been such a long winded affair that I didn't want anymore problems. I'd have agreed to anything just so Susie and I could get away. Susie had already told me about the Department's attitude to Brumby Leeke, the owner of Prairie Downs, so I wasn't going to get into a fight over that one.

We were happy to leave Moore River, but sad too. I was anxious to get away and have a bit of freedom, but sad to leave all my new friends behind, as well as Jack and Jean. Susie was looking forward to station work. She wanted to get as far away from Neville as possible. She reckoned he was so nosey he even knew when you were going to the toilet.

All our friends and relatives were crying when we left. I was crying myself, but knew it was a better life we were going to than the one we'd had there. If Jack had've been able to let me know what Moore River was like beforehand I would never have gone there in the first place.

108

9

An Opportunity Lost
1933-1935

Billy Martin was a good bloke, a real Australian. He'd been to war, he was honest and hard working and a gentleman. He trusted you. It didn't worry him to go away and leave Susie and me in charge. There were only two other permanent workers on Mt Padbury then, Georgy, who was an uncle of Susie's in the tribal way, and a young Englishman, who wasn't that experienced in station work.

The country around there was flat, except for Mt Padbury of course, which was the hill after which the station had been named. It was good grazing country, especially for horses. While Susie was cooking I was mustering sheep, looking after cattle, fencing and doing a bit of horse-breaking. My pay was around two quid a week.

The horse-breaking reminded me of my days with old Harry Farber, the greatest horse-breaker of them all. Horse-breaking is hard work and you can make it harder by not doing certain things properly. For example, if you don't mouth them the right way, if you let them take the bit in their teeth, you can pull them as much as you like later on and it won't affect them at all.

Once I had the headstall on them I'd let them roll around in the yard for a day or two, while they got used to it. While one horse was relaxing you go out and catch another one, so you end up with a few horses on the go all the time, but at different stages. That way you're not sitting around doing nothing in between.

Of course they all love to chuck you off, that's part of the game, but you can't let them beat you. You have to get back on and have another go. They'll try all sorts of tricks like running you into the fence. You just have to ignore all that business and keep going with them. They come good as long as you're patient.

There were a lot of Top Rail Riders around stations in those days. They all treated the whole thing as a bit of a joke. They loved it when you got a real mean bugger because you'd be on and off the horse all the time and they thought it was real funny.

Most horses only take about a week's working, mean ones a bit longer. A mean horse will always have piggy eyes. That sounds funny, but that's how you pick them. If their eyes look piggy, and they're watching you all the time in a real sly way, you know you've got a mean bugger.

I shouldn't complain about horses really because mules are much worse. Mules are stubborn and take a long time to get used to you. You never want to ride an unbroken mule into the bush on your own because you'll never know when you'll be coming back. You hop off a mule and he'll pull aside, jump, kick you and all. With a horse you just have to watch their head and go with them, the same way you do when you're riding a bike, but a mule is different, they can surprise you. I often thought I was finally getting somewhere with a mule and would then find out quick smart that I was not.

I had been working for Billy for a few months when a letter arrived from Neville. It said they'd checked their records and couldn't find Billy's permit to employ me and Susie. They said it was illegal for him to employ natives like us without a permit. They sent him a form which he had to fill in and return before he would be allowed to keep me and Susie there. Billy showed me the letter and it made me really angry. I had never heard of this permit system before, what did they think we were, dogs that needed licensing?

I wrote to Mr Neville and told him that I could do station work without him interfering and that I would not work under a permit. I was old enough to look after myself.

Billy got some men together after that and we went on a droving trip to Noreena Downs Station. I took Susie into Meekatharra before we left because she was due to have our first child, and Meekatharra Hospital had started letting a few Aborigines in.

We were six weeks on the road on that trip. Two weeks going up and four weeks coming back with four thousand head of sheep.

110

I was the cook and no one died so I don't suppose I did too badly.

On our way home to Mt Padbury something funny happened. We pulled in at a well to water the sheep and decided to camp there. I was getting some tea ready when Tom Broad, who was pulling the water, sang out, 'Hey Jack! Come and look at this sign someone's nailed up here.'

'I've got enough to do without looking at that', I replied. 'I've got meat and damper on the fire, I can't leave it now.'

'I'll read it to you then, you might find it funny, it's about your old boss Farber.'

'Righto, I'm listening.'

'Goodnight Midnight Harry, and all your kicking bastards and mules, if there was a mongrel I ever met, you're the only one of them!'

We laughed and laughed. I could imagine someone writing that about Harry.

On that same trip I met Brumby Leeke. Susie had told me quite a lot about him by then. He had sent her money when she was at the Settlement and wanted her to go back north to his station. Her mother had wanted Susie back too, but of course Neville wouldn't agree. Neville had this idea that Brumby had taken advantage of Susie when she was younger, but Susie said it wasn't true. Anyway, Brumby came up to me where we were camped and said, 'You Jack McPhee?'

'Yes.'

'I'm Brumby Leeke. I'm in this area droving too. I hear you're married to a girl called Mularna.'

'Yes, I think so. What's her white name?'

'Bessie Connaughton, she's like a daughter to me.'

'Yes, that name's right, but they changed it at the Settlement to Susie Smith. She's in hospital right now having a baby.'

'You don't say? Well, any time you want to come over to Prairie Downs there's a place for you. I've got horses and cattle, you're welcome to come and live there permanently.'

Once we hit Mt Padbury we stayed a few days to settle the sheep down and then went into Meekatharra. I picked up Susie and baby Marie. She was a good healthy baby, and we all came back with Billy on the truck.

When I told Susie about meeting Brumby she was very excited. All she wanted to do after that was go and see her mother, who was on Bulloo Downs at the time, and Brumby.

After a while Brumby wrote and let us know that should we come to Prairie Downs he'd like to leave the station to us after he died. That was it as far as Susie was concerned, she didn't want to stay another minute on Mt Padbury. She was a strong woman and once she got an idea into her head it was hard to do anything with her.

I wasn't sure what to do myself, despite Susie urging me to take Brumby up on his offer. I knew it was a wonderful opportunity for both of us, and he struck me as the sort of bloke who wouldn't make a suggestion like that unless he really meant it. I had promised Neville I would never take Susie to Prairie Downs and I knew that somehow word would get back to him if I just went there and didn't tell him. In the end I thought it might be best to be open about the whole thing, tell him what we were doing, but also tell him about Brumby's offer to leave the station to us. Surely he wouldn't want us to miss out on an opportunity like that. I also added in the letter I sent that I still didn't like working under a permit, just in case he got the idea of sending Brumby one of those forms as well.

We said goodbye to Billy Martin and left Mt Padbury towards the end of 1933. Billy was happy for us, 'Best of luck Jack', he said, 'you'll do well there, Old Brum is a bit too old to handle all that on his own now.

We hitched a lift with Campbell and Co., they carted mail and one thing and another up to Marble Bar by truck. They dropped us off at Bulloo Downs, which was on the way to Prairie Downs, because that's as far as they were going at that time.

That suited us perfectly as Susie was anxious to see her mother, Piper, and show her the baby. It had been nine years since they'd seen each other so you can imagine how excited they all were. We told her what our plans were and Piper decided she would like to come to Prairie Downs with us.

Watty Hall, the boss at Bulloo Downs, came and met me. He'd heard what was going on and said, 'I don't know whether Brum is at the homestead just now and I haven't got enough spare horses to give you all one each to ride over there. If you can ride over on your own and let him know you're here, he'll come over in the buggy and pick you all up.'

That's exactly what we did, and we were soon all living happily on Prairie Downs.

Susie was pleased to be with Brum and the other people there. Some of the old women living on the station had nursed her as a child, so they were very pleased to see her back and with her own baby too. There were more Aboriginal people than I expected on Prairie Downs, they liked to hang around and work for Brum because he fed them better than the other squatters and made sure they were looked after properly.

After we'd been there a few weeks Brum and I had a talk and he told me his version of why they took Susie away in the first place.

Susie's father had been Billy Connaughton, a whiteman of all trades, who'd been living with Piper, Susie's mother, who was a ngayarda banujutha. When Billy passed away, Piper had moved onto Prairie Downs and lived with Brumby. When Susie had grown into a teenager there was an Aboriginal bloke there who tribally was her straight nyuba. It meant he had a right to take Susie as his wife. Brum wasn't keen on her marrying tribally because she was mardamarda and had been brought up differently. Her tribal nyuba was cross that Brum would not let her go, so he got some of his mates together and they decided to take care of Brum and then steal Susie away.

They waited until Brum went into the station store and then jammed him in there. While two guards stood outside, the other two tried to beat him up. The only thing that saved him was the shotgun he had hidden in there, he grabbed it and shot the bloke who wanted Susie, in the leg. The police heard about what had happened and came out to investigate. The tribal blokes made false statements saying they'd seen Brum sleeping with Susie on the verandah. She would have only been fourteen at the time. After that Susie was sent to Moore River.

Besides listening to Brum's side of the story I kept my ear out for gossip. Many of the same people were still on the station and they all knew what had happened. I knew that if the story Brum had told me wasn't true, one of them would let slip something. You could always count on the Mulba grapevine for things like that, and those old people have wonderful memories. There was nothing, not a thing. According to them, Brum's story was right, so I set my mind at rest over it.

Brum confided to me that he was worried that the Aborigines Department might still cause us some trouble. He was in his seventies then and past the stage of being interested in molesting anyone, but he reckoned the Department wouldn't believe that. He decided to take up some land out on the Oakover and put it in my name so that if worse came to worst we would at least have that. He took up a pastoral lease of sixty-four thousand acres for us near Balfour Downs country.

About the same time I talked to Brum about my cousin Jack Doherty and his wife Jean. I explained about Jack's eyesight but Brum said he was quite happy to have them come and live with us. He was sure there'd be something they could do around the station. I wrote to Jack and sent him ten quid for the train fare and expenses to get them to Meekatharra, I was going to ride in and pick them up from there. I wanted Jack out of the Settlement, it was no life for him.

A few weeks later I received a letter from Jack to say that he was temporarily keeping the money I had sent as Neville would not give permission for them to leave Moore River and join me because I was defying the Department by living on Prairie Downs.

I was really disappointed, because I had been looking forward to being with Jack again. As far as I was concerned all the Aborigines Department gave you was trouble, nothing else. They had already forced Piper to return to Bulloo Downs, because her man refused to work with her away. That had been a great disappointment to Susie as she had wanted her mother to be able to stay with us for good. And now, instead of letting Jack and Jean have a go at a better life, they were refusing to let them leave simply because of me. That was the whole trouble with them, they treated you like an ignorant child. They wanted to be able to dictate your own life to you.

Not long after that Brum got a letter from Neville warning him not to let me and Susie stay on Prairie Downs. Brum showed me

A.O. Neville. (Battye 20183P5000B)

the letter and said, 'As far as I'm concerned Jack, I've never seen this bloody letter!' Then he threw it away.

I wrote to Neville asking him to let us stay. I told him we were very happy and didn't want to leave. I asked him who else would employ me for three pounds a week plus keep. Also, I explained to him again that one day the station would be ours, that I was already a boss there, and that it was a wonderful opportunity for us to get on in the world.

What I didn't know then was that Neville had already issued a warrant through the Commissioner of Police for Susie to be taken from me and sent back to Moore River. You see, I thought that because she was a married woman with one child and another on the way, they wouldn't go that far. I thought she belonged to me, not them. I was wrong.

In November of 1934 Susie had our son Johnny in Meekatharra Hospital. I was very pleased to have a boy because I thought then that when I died I could leave Prairie Downs to my son.

Not long after Christmas, in early 1935, the policeman from Peak Hill Station came out to see us.

'Unless the three of you take heed of this warning', he told us, 'I will have to enforce the warrant for the removal of Mrs Susie McPhee to Moore River Settlement. Unless Jack and Susie leave here, Brumby, the warrant will come into effect.'

'I'm not going to fire him', said Brum, 'I don't look on him as a native, I don't treat him as a native, therefore I'm not doing anything wrong by employing him'.

The policeman took me and Susie aside and asked quietly how we were being treated.

'Good', I told him, 'he's happy to have us here and we're happy to be here. We're family to him, he's made me a boss already and wants us to have the place when he's gone. Can't you just leave us alone?'

'Are you sure he has no dishonourable intentions towards your wife?'

'Look at him', I pointed to Brum, 'he's a done man, what's he going to get up to?'

The policeman looked at Brum and had to admit that he didn't look too good.

116

'I'm sorry', he said, 'but there's nothing I can do, you have to obey these orders, you're a native!'

'I'm not a native!! I've lived and worked with whitemen all my life, I've even eaten with them, Mr Neville knows that. Susie's my wife, we've got two kids, we were legally married, how can he have more say over where she goes than me?'

'Because you're both natives, you're not whites. You have to do as he says, he's your Protector.'

I laughed at that one. I was so angry, I thought of all the times when me and different ones I knew could have done with a bit of protection, and where was he then? Nowhere! And now here he was, interfering with the best offer I'd ever had. If Neville was going to protect us at all, it should have been from bad, not good!

The policeman ended up warning us all once more and then leaving. He said he would put his report in but if we weren't gone in a week he would have to come out and get Susie.

We were all very, very upset. Brum was all for defying Neville, but I knew Susie couldn't handle going back to the Settlement. I decided we would have to leave. I wrote to Neville telling him that we were going, but that as far as I was concerned he had done us a very bad turn and I would not forget it.

Brum was his usual generous self when we left. He gave us a wagon full of stores, two camels, twenty-five head of cattle and twelve head of horses.

'At least you've got that bit of land', he told us, 'if you fall on hard times and those horses get run down, sneak back here and I'll give you a fresh lot. I'll be able to help that way as long as that bastard Neville doesn't get wind of it.'

10
Struggling To Earn A Living
1935-1938

When we left Prairie Downs we took Punch with us. He was the old blackfella who'd been with me in the early days with Harry Farber, and was now working for Brum. Also, Harry, Larry, Smoker and a couple of others came too. Most of them were lads from the Ashburton area, and the idea was that they would work with me on my land, helping me to set up my own station.

My land was about two hundred miles from Prairie Downs so I figured it would take us around three weeks to get there. Marie was only a couple of years old and Johnny was still a baby, so I had to think of them a little bit in the travelling.

The land Brum had taken up for us was near the edge of the desert and it was good country, as long as it rained. If it didn't rain, you were really stuck because the country got dry very, very quickly and that was no good for the horses, who were our main work animals.

As we travelled further and further on we came across more and more tribal people coming in from the desert. Some of them had never had contact with white people but they would come in with others who had been in before and stay for up to six months in the Nullagine area. They never wore any clothes coming in, but they were always dressed going back out again.

It was these tribal people from the Rudall River area that gave me problems with my lads. You see, the trouble was that the fellas with me came from what they considered civilised country, and seeing wild blackfellas come in from what they thought was wild country frightened them. What made it even worse was the rumour that had been going around that one of these wild blacks was an albino. I knew it was more than just a rumour because he had actually been sighted by different people, but I didn't see that this mattered. For some reason, the lads with me took it into their heads that he was devil-devil and had magic powers. They talked about this over and over and made themselves very frightened. They thought that being an albino might make him an even stronger devil-devil man; who knows what he might be able to do?

Around the campfire one night I tried to explain to them all that he was just a human being and wasn't going to do them any harm. I also pointed out that none of them had even seen the man, so what were they getting all worked up about.

'We don't need to see him', they said, 'we know he's here, maybe over in those bushes hiding somewhere, could be anywhere round here, could do anything to us too!' It didn't matter what I said or how I explained it, they wouldn't let go of that devil-devil idea.

When I got up the next morning they'd all gone, slipped away during the night, even Old Punch. The thought of the devil-devil was just too much for them.

This left me in a terrible spot because I had the cattle, the wagon, the horses, Susie and the two kids. There was no way we could possibly go on alone. I decided the only sensible thing to do was turn around and head back in.

I took charge of the cart and camels and Marie. Susie took charge of the horses and Johnny. We left the cattle to run free. You can imagine how hard it was trying to manage everything and having two tiny kids as well.

On the way in we came to a creek that was running pretty full. I scouted up and down but there was no better crossing so we decided to cross there. As I moved the wagon into the creek the wheel hit a rock and smashed, the wagon went over on one side and Marie and I flew into the water. I leapt up and fished Marie out, fortunately she hadn't hit her head or anything, she was just soaking wet and upset.

I righted the wagon and checked the wheel, there was no way I could repair it, I never had the proper tools and it needed new spokes. I felt really down, it was stinking hot, the kids were crying and I just felt like giving up.

Also, I couldn't help thinking that if it hadn't been for Neville we'd all be safe and well on Prairie Downs. I sat down for a spell and decided the best thing was to pack all the gear from the wagon onto the camels and head for the nearest station where I might be able to get a bit of help.

We crossed the creek with the horses and camels and ended up camping just before Quinpen Spring. Susie and I talked it over and decided it was just too difficult struggling on with the horses, so we thought we would make a water trough and leave them there until we could come back for them, which hopefully would only be a few days. The next morning we dug a well in the sand and shored it up with timber. I made a makeshift trough and filled it with water for the horses. Then we took the two camels and two riding horses and headed for Meetheena Station.

When we arrived at Meetheena I saw the manager and hired a paddock off him. I decided to stay there for a few days and rest before I headed back for the horses.

To my surprise, Jack and Jean were there, Neville had finally given them permission to leave and they had been trying to contact me so we could all live together on my land. It was wonderful to see him again, it really cheered me up. Also, a lot of my other relatives were on Meetheena at that time, including my Aunty Dinah, so it was just the medicine I needed.

After a few days I thought I should go out and bring my horses in. I rounded them up and camped at Quinpen Spring. It's what they call a night spring, during the day you would never know there was water there, but as soon as the sun goes down it comes bubbling up and you can drink as much as you like.

I watered my horses and hobbled them out, made myself a bit of tucker and then looked round for a good place to sleep.

I saw a bit of a mound on the ground and I thought it would make a good pillow, so I rested my head on that and went to sleep. I normally sleep good in the bush but that night was terrible. Something kept coming and scratching me on the head. I'd brush it away and it would come back and scratch me again.

When I woke up the next morning I felt really buggered. I got to Meetheena that night, it was only thirty miles from Quinpen, and put my horses in my paddock. Then I went down to the family and had some tucker. While we were all sitting around there I told my relatives about what an awful night I'd had.

'What do you think it was?', I asked them. They all laughed their heads off.

'That pillow was your old cousin's grave', they said, 'he was buried there over twenty-five years ago. He was just saying hello to you!'

I stayed for three weeks on Meetheena until the wool truck came out, then I got a lift into the Bar to see if I could get parts for my broken wagon wheel. The blacksmith there gave me some of his tools and new spokes. I managed to hitch another lift back to Meetheena and told Jack that I was going to head out to my wagon and try and fix the wheel.

'It'll be easier if two of us go', he said, 'then when we all leave here we can all do something together'.

That sounded like a good idea to me and it meant that Jack and I could have a good yarn on our own away from the women.

We took two camels with us but decided not to ride them because we knew walking would take longer and we wanted to have a real good natter and make plans about what we'd like to do together. In those days it was nothing to walk hundreds of miles, as long as you paced yourself, knew the country, and had food and water. Jack and I both knew that area well. There was no danger of anything happening to us, though it could be hard for other men to survive out there.

We found the wagon exactly where I had left it. Over the next few days we tried to fix the wheel but we were just hopeless at it, so we collected up all the broken bits and walked into Eastern Creek. I'd heard there was a fella in there who was good with wheels. He fixed it for us no worries at all, we never told him how we'd spent days working on the damn thing.

It was wonderful to have the wheel fixed, but it left us with another problem; how were we going to transport a whacking great wagon wheel back to the cart?

'We'll have to think about this one', I said to Jack. 'It's a bit tricky.'

We both sat down and looked at the camels. Those bloody great humps, you couldn't balance a wheel on that. Also, we only had one wheel not two, we couldn't strap the wheel to one side of the camel because he'd fall over, two wheels would have been different. We couldn't tie the wheel between the camels either, because they wouldn't be able to walk in step and it would just lead to an accident.

Finally I said, 'I've got it!'

We got some empty petrol cases and fastened them to the camel around his saddle, then we slowly packed up the sides with different things until the hump was cleared. Jack and I cut some saplings and made a frame, we tied that onto the top of everything else and lifted the wheel up and tied it on top of the frame. It took us quite a while to balance it properly, you have to get it just right or it's too hard for the poor old camel.

We finally got it balanced and set off back to the wagon, which was thirty miles away. We fixed the wheel on and then drove back to Meetheena Station, where we all spent a few days talking over what we should do.

Jack and I agreed that it was getting too dry to go out to my land now, especially with young children and with horses who were used to grazing country, not spinifex. We decided to fill in with prospecting until after the rain had come, and then we would think about my land again.

We left Meetheena and prospected around Lyndon, which is about fifty miles from Nullagine township. Although we worked hard we didn't seem to find much and it was a very hard life for the women. Susie had to go out bush with the kids to shoot a roo so we had something to eat at night. She worked very, very hard, as hard as a man, and I admired her for it. Eventually, Jack took a job helping another prospector, I lent him one of my camels and he used to cart stone for him. We all wanted to stay together, but it was becoming harder and harder to do so. I could see that eventually we would have to split up.

It was during my time at Lyndon that I met up with Ted Greig, who was to become a good friend of mine. Ted was a very good prospector and spent a lot of his time working the gold belt around Nullagine. The gold belt was about eighty miles long and fifteen miles wide, and any prospector worth his salt knew that if you went too far either side of that the gold just petered out.

I've never met anyone who was as good as Ted. He was so good people used to say he could smell gold. I thought very highly of him because he was what I call a real dinkum Australian. He mixed with Chinese, Afghans, anyone, he didn't care. He treated everyone the same. If he did make a criticism of someone it was always in a jokey way and no one got offended.

As far as I knew Ted never had any family, only his old cattle dog Micky. He really loved that dog. He'd make up a big stew for the two of them and when he'd had his share he would let Micky polish off the rest. That dog would lick the camp oven so clean Ted would say there was no point in washing it twice. I knew quite a few people who had dog dishwashers in those days.

Ted was a whiteman, but he had an Aboriginal name too, Wallabong. It meant bloody liar! He'd been given that name years before by the people on Warralong Station. Ted had strung them all along with a lot of tall stories and when they finally cottoned on to him they decided to change his name to Wallabong. Everyone loved him, he was just such a good natured man. Even white people called him Wallabong. It just sort of stuck to him.

Ted gave me a lot of advice about prospecting and helped out whenever I needed a hand with digging and so on.

After we'd been around Lyndon for six months I decided that it wasn't worth staying and that we would have to think about moving somewhere else. Jack and Jean agreed with me, they took another temporary job cooking and cleaning at someone else's mine, but that only lasted a few weeks and then they decided to move back down to Perth. They thought it might be easier for them to find work there, especially with Jack's eyes being so bad.

Susie was about due with our third child, Josie, by then and I wanted her to be near a doctor just in case she needed help. I arranged for her to go and stay at the One Mile, it was an area of land one mile from the Port Hedland town boundary where mardamarda people were allowed to live. It wasn't an official government reserve, but I suppose it was as good as. Dr Vickers came out and delivered the baby when she was due, at that time Aboriginal people still weren't allowed in Port Hedland Hospital. I think Dr Vickers would have been happy to have Aboriginal patients in there, but there were too many people opposed to the idea for him to get it changed. It was 1936 by then, and I was beginning to wonder how I was going to support a wife and three young children with no money coming in.

I got to thinking about my land again and my dream to have a station of my own one day. I knew I could do it, I was a hard worker and there wasn't anything I couldn't do on a station. I just needed a helping hand from nature, no interference from the government and a bit of luck.

There'd been a small amount of rain so I thought I might try mustering. It was a good opportunity for me to go out and check the conditions on my land, because I knew Susie and the kids were being well looked after at the One Mile. I rounded up some blokes who were able and willing to give me a hand, Micky, Jacky Aspro, and a couple of others, and out we went.

With cattle it's important to let them know they belong to someone. If you don't let cattle know you're about and leave them alone too long, say three or four years, they go wild. Then, when you want to muster and brand, it makes your job a little bit harder. We rounded up as many as we could, branded them and let them go.

There hadn't been enough rain for us to stay out there too long, but at least we let the cattle know we were around.

I had been hoping to bring some in to sell, but there wasn't enough feed or water on the country at that time. It meant I couldn't get them in healthy enough to get a decent price. That's why I let them free range. I thought after the next lot of rain I might have a better chance of getting them in in a healthy condition.

On the way back in from my land who should we come across but my old boss Harry Farber. He recognised me straight away and said, 'Good to see you Jack, you look well'.

'Oh yes', I said, 'I'm getting older, but you're worse off because you're even older than me!'

'Yes', he said, 'and down and out too. I'm trying to get a few bob together for my family, they're at Mullewa. I've lost all my sheep. I was droving and left some Englishman in charge and they let the lot go. I'm trying to see if I can round up some of them, I've got no insurance on those sheep. You haven't seen any sign of them around this area have you?'

'No sign of sheep at all, and we've just been all through this country. The only animals we've seen besides cattle are dingoes.'

'So what have you been doing?'

'I've just finished branding, I'm heading back in now to go prospecting.'

'I hear the Comet mine is doing well.'

'I can't tell you much about that one. Probably just making tucker money, but I suppose that's better than nothing these days.'

We parted then, and I have to say I felt really sorry for him. If I had've seen even a hint of sheep I'd have given him a hand to get them in. I never kept any ill feeling towards him after that. As far as I was concerned the past was done with and I think he felt the same. You can't keep going on and on forever about things. It's like boiling the same cabbage over and over, after a while it starts to stink and you can't stomach it anymore.

I never went back to Lyndon, it wasn't any good. I moved in a bit closer towards Nullagine and did a bit of dry blowing. Susie came out with the kids and joined me, but it was still a very hard life for us all.

Prospecting is more suited to a single man, a married man's a mug to take it up. The trouble is you never know if you're going to find gold today, tomorrow or next year, but you can always count on the kids wanting and needing things every day. It just wasn't a reliable enough job.

I went into Nullagine town to see if I could hunt up a different kind of work and while I was there I got into trouble with the Aborigines Department again. The policeman said to me, 'You're Jack McPhee, aren't you?'

'Yes.'

'I've had a report that you own land and stock.'

'Yes.'

'Do you have any rights?'

'What rights?'

'Are you exempt from the Native Affairs Act?'

'I don't know, I don't think so.'

'Have you ever been given an Exemption Certificate?'

'No.'

'Well Jack, that means you've got no rights according to the laws of this country. Because you're a native it's illegal for you to own land or stock. You can only have those things if you're made exempt by the government. You see, if you're granted an Exemption Certificate, it puts you on the same level as a whiteman. It means you can do these things and not get into trouble. I think you'd better put in for it, you strike me as the kind of bloke who wants to get on in the world, and you won't without it.'

The policeman went on to explain to me that having an Exemption might also make a difference to the wages I was paid if I ended up working for someone. You see, in those days people could pay blackmen whatever they liked and get away with it. Some were never paid at all. It was either cheap labour or free labour in those days.

I told the policeman that I would have to think about it because I just couldn't see why it was necessary. Why did I need an Exemption Certificate simply because I was a different colour? It made no sense to me at all. You could tell it was the government's idea, they were always thinking of things that didn't make any sense.

While I was in Nullagine I heard a rumour about a thing you could apply for called Maternity Allowance. I thought I might be able to apply for it for Susie for our last child. I made some enquiries about it and was told I'd have a much better chance of getting it if I had an Exemption Certificate.

It seemed I couldn't get away from that bloody certificate, so in the end I decided to write to Mr Neville and offer to buy one from him. I asked him to write and tell me how much an Exemption cost and I would forward the money to him.

I received a reply a few weeks later, Susie and I were still prospecting and undecided about where we should move to. Neville said he was looking into an Exemption for me but that I owed the Department three pounds from when they looked after Susie. Apparently, I was liable for the bill because I was her husband. They said the money was for her board when she was in the East Perth Girls Home and for a train fare that she'd once had coming back from a job in the country. Three pounds at that time was like a million dollars to me. I wrote and told him I would pay when I could.

Neville then wrote to me again and said before he could grant me an Exemption I had to meet certain requirements. He advised me to go into Nullagine and see the policeman there, as I had to fill out a form before they would consider me.

I went and saw Mick Liddlelow, who was the policeman in Nullagine, and he was very helpful. He helped me with the form and explained it all. He told me that if my Exemption was granted I had to promise not to do certain things. I wasn't allowed to associate with ngayarda banujutha Aborigines, I wasn't allowed to live in a native camp, I wasn't allowed to take part in a corroboree, I wasn't even allowed to associate with any Aboriginal people who didn't have an Exemption. In return, the government would allow me to have drinking rights, as long as I showed my Exemption if I was asked for it. I would be allowed to buy and sell stock and land, and I would be on the same standard as a whiteman. He also said, though, that if I broke any of my promises I could easily lose my Exemption, in which case I would become a native again.

Out of all those things what really got me was the bit about corroborees. I had such fond memories of dancing with no clothes on, of being painted and decorated, of hearing the women and men singing. I couldn't see anything wrong with that at all. It meant that I had to give away all that my mother belonged to. I felt upset about that. I didn't think I should have to make a choice, but I agreed to it all because I wanted something better for my family, and at the time that seemed the only way to get it.

Mick also said to me, 'You know, for white people Jack is short for John, it's like a nickname. If you're granted this Exemption it might be good for you to use the name John in your business dealings. It might get you more respect.'

'Thank you for mentioning that Mick', I said, 'I'll do that'. And so from then on for anything official or to do with business I went by the name John McPhee.

Not long after they sent my application in I received another letter from Neville asking me to send him references about my character. That stuck in my throat. I didn't see why I needed references, I ignored his letter and wrote to him instead telling him details of the land and stock I owned. I thought when he read that it would be enough. I was wrong, he replied asking me why I hadn't sent any references.

In the end I got Mick Liddlelow, Constable Mounter from Port Hedland and Mr Meehan from Austin Downs Station to write me references and forward them to Neville.

I followed that up with a letter saying, 'You asked me for two references and I've given you three good ones, more than what you asked for. Can I please have my Exemption?'

Susie and I were fed up with prospecting by then so we decided to move into Port Hedland and live at the One Mile while I tried to find some work there. I was trying to raise some cash just in case there were any fees for my Exemption.

I went and saw the Harbour and Light Department in Hedland to see if I could get a job on the wharf. I'd heard the pay was quite good for that kind of work.

When I applied they said, 'We don't hire niggers here, you better get going!' That made me really wild, but there was no point in getting into a fight over it, so I just walked away.

I scouted around a bit more and finally got a job working in Len Taplin's garage.

Everyone in Hedland had to live by the curfew then. All Aboriginal people had to be out of town by six o'clock or you could be gaoled. The only ones allowed to stay later were those washing dishes and things like that.

While I was working for Len my Exemption came through. Dr Vickers sent word that he wanted to see me, I went and saw him after work and he said, 'I've got your Exemption Jack, you're not under the Native Affairs anymore, you can have a drink in the pub now'.

I signed the form to say I'd received it and then set off for home. I knew it wasn't really important, I knew I was still the same Jack McPhee, but I have to admit, it did make me feel a bit gamer.

We continued to live at the One Mile for a few more months and while we were there Neville sent the police to check on me. You see he was worried I wasn't keeping my side of the bargain. I wasn't supposed to be associating with other Aborigines now I was a whiteman. The thing was, there was a shortage of housing in Hedland then, it was hard enough for whites to find a place let alone blacks. Also, the mob that lived on One Mile were very well behaved and they were all hard workers, I didn't see any problem at all, but Neville obviously did. Finally Dr Vickers wrote to him and said he thought it was a suitable place for me to live and no reason to cancel my Exemption.

My job at the garage ran out but I'd managed to save a bit of money by then and Clancy Doherty had been to see me and said he'd found a good patch of gold. He wanted us to become partners. That sounded as good a proposition as any, so I bought some stores and we all moved out to Boodalarie, which is about fifty miles from Nullagine.

It wasn't a bad show, there was gold in the rock and we used to break it into small pieces and cart it into the battery for crushing. We worked on rough measurements in those days, thirty-two pebbles in an old prospector's kerosene bucket weighed about one ton. It was very slow work, we only had one good working camel, so Clancy and I would take turns carting the stone to the battery.

I remember one day we were in our camp when we saw these two wild camels coming in. Susie was very frightened of camels, she didn't want me to go near them, but I knew if I could catch one it would make our work easier.

I pointed to the second camel and said, 'He looks friendly, I wonder if I could get him?'

'He'll bite you', Susie said.

'No, I think I can get that fella.' I started slowly towards them. The one who was a real wild bull camel spotted me and took off. The other one went to run but I sang out to him and he stopped. I kept on talking quietly to him until I was close enough to reach out and put my hand on his shoulder. He was mine after that. I called out to Susie to bring me a halter and I put it on him. Clancy made a saddle for him later, he was very clever that way.

We continued to crush dirt and ended up getting an ounce of gold for every ton crushed. Gold was only about nine quid an ounce then, but it was enough to keep the billy boiling. After a while the gold we could easily get at ran out so we decided to move closer in to Cookes Creek, which was only forty miles from Nullagine. We managed to find eighteen ounces of gold around that area, but we found that by the time we paid for the crushing and our stores we didn't have much left over.

We had been at Cookes Creek a few months when we got word Brumby Leeke had died and been buried. It took a long time for news to reach us because we were so isolated. I was disappointed that I had missed his funeral because he had done his best by us, and if it hadn't been for Neville, he would have done more. Prairie Downs was sold up after he died and I tried not to think about it. It only made me angry.

While we were at Cookes Creek a policeman was sent out to check on our living conditions. Somehow Neville had got word that I was associating with Aborigines. To tell you the truth, I had been. I often had other Mulbas around my camp. They'd call in, stay a few days and leave. Some of them were my friends and relations and I was just being friendly like anyone would. Luckily they'd all gone when the policeman came out so there was only Clancy, me and Susie.

The policeman said he'd send back a report saying my living conditions were all right, but unfortunately he mentioned that Clancy and I were partners. Neville did some checking and found out that Clancy didn't have his Exemption Certificate. He'd had one years ago but they'd taken it from him for giving a drink to a friend and even though he'd re-applied for it a couple of times since then, they kept knocking him back.

This got me into more trouble because Neville sent me a letter saying that I shouldn't associate with Clancy, let alone share a business with him. Clancy was like a brother to me, I found that very hard to take. Neville said that unless Clancy and I split up he would cancel my Exemption.

I decided the best thing to do was to ignore his letter for a while. The next time we took a load into the twenty-mile battery for crushing, Simpson, the battery manager, said to me, 'Look Jack, we can't go on crushing you and Clancy's gold under someone else's name. If we get caught there'll be trouble. Why don't you get your own Miner's Rights?'

'Well, I tried a few years ago, they wouldn't give it to me', I explained.

'Let me see what I can do, I might be able to wangle it some way.'

I agreed to this because I knew Simpson was a Justice of the Peace and might be able to pull it off. Within a few weeks he had my Miner's Rights for me, I was really pleased, it made the whole thing so much simpler.

We continued to prospect and Neville continued to threaten me over Clancy. In the end Neville won, because the gold ran out again and Clancy and I decided to separate. Susie was sick of living so far out. She worried about the kids getting sick or being bitten by a snake. She reckoned that we were so far away from help that we'd be dead by the time we got it. We decided to pack up and move in next to the twenty-mile battery, which was only twenty miles from Nullagine town.

We set up our tents and fly in our new camp, and to make it a bit nicer I built a great big bough-shed over the whole thing to keep out the rain and sun.

There was talk of war breaking out even then and people were wondering if Australia would get involved. I had already decided that I would try and join up if it came to that, but I never said anything to Susie, I knew she wouldn't want me going anywhere.

11

Finding A Better Way
1939-1941

I hunted around and got work with a contractor, driving his Ford
V8 truck. I had to cart twenty-five ton of stone a day from the
All Nations mine to be crushed at the Barton mine, which was
about four miles away. I did five loads a day and it was bloody
hard work. By this time I was willing to take on any work at
all just to put a few bob in our pockets.

Now and then the Barton hired me to do the odd job too. They
had a problem one day with water in the shaft and they asked
me to help out. Des Corboy and I had to climb down a one hundred
and twenty foot shaft. We were mucking around with a pump at
the bottom and were up and down all day, it was a big job.

In the afternoon I stayed down too long. I should have kept
coming up for air like Des did now and then but I was that stuck
into the job I just forgot about it. Around seven o'clock that night
we finished. Des went up first and I followed him. However as
soon as I reached the top of the shaft the fresh air hit me and
I went out to it. Luckily, Doug Gallop was standing nearby and
he just managed to grab me under the arm as I started to fall,
he sang out to Des and he ran over and they both hauled me
out. They saved my life. If it hadn't been for them I would've fallen
back down the shaft and been killed.

I continued to cart stone and fill in with other jobs on weekends
too. I was becoming very dissatisfied with the contractor because
in the weeks I'd been working he hadn't paid me a penny. I'd asked
him about it, but he just kept saying, 'Oh you'll get your bloody

money, stop worrying!'

I never liked being in debt to anyone, and because he wasn't paying me I had to keep booking all our food up, otherwise the family would have starved.

The other thing I wasn't happy about was the fact that he expected me to do all the repairs on his truck. He never serviced it once. The brakes were lousy and there was a hill I had to go up and down. I had to drive very, very carefully. After three months' solid work and not a penny in wages, I decided to chuck it in. I was a bloody fool to have stayed that long, but I suppose I kept hoping he'd come good. I didn't know what to do then, no job, kids to feed, in debt, I was desperate.

I went and saw Simpson, the battery manager at the twenty-mile, and told him what had happened. I asked if there was any work at all he could give me. He said, 'Well, there's not much going here, but at least you'll get paid for what you do and I can give you an advance till work builds up a bit'. I started work that day.

The following day that contractor who robbed me came out and saw me.

'What's the matter Jack, why have you left the truck?'

'You don't pay nothin'', I told him, 'I'm flogging my guts out and getting nothing for it! You drive around Nullagine all day in your bloody flash car chasing women, while my kids are going hungry because of you. Your brakes are shot, you're no good. Why do you think I left your bloody truck?!'

Then Simpson came over and said to him, 'You're just a mongrel, treating a man like that! No money and a family to feed. If I was younger I'd give you a bloody good hiding for what you've done!' He got in his car and took off after that, I never ever got a cent from him.

The battery work was contract work, as a lot of work was in those days. It wasn't an easy way to live because it meant you had to make the money you earnt last till the next job.

There were two main jobs at the battery, bogging, which was shovelling cyanide sand, or feeding the battery. Feeding the battery was more irregular because you were always waiting on prospectors to bring dirt in. If there wasn't enough ore to crush they used to shut the battery down.

133

My first job there was bogging, I worked with Scotty Munro, a whitefella. He had to fill and empty three of the thirty-six-ton vats there, and I was contracted to do the other three. We were paid six quid a vat, three quid to empty and three quid to fill. It was only possible to do three a week because then you had to wait three weeks for them to leach. While they were leaching I had to find other work. Scotty used to amaze me because I prided myself on being a good worker, but sometimes he even used to beat me. He didn't look like a really strong bloke, but by gee, he was good with that shovel. He just seemed to have the right knack for it. It was very easy to do your back in shovelling, and my back used to hurt often, but Scotty was never worried about that. When I think of all the dirt I've shovelled in my life I laugh. I couldn't shovel shit from a sick duck now!

The other good thing about working at the battery was Wallabong, Ted Greig, my prospecting mate. He often worked there tidying up and feeding the silver into the box. He was very good at that, he would look at the plates and be able to judge exactly how much silver was needed. Ted was a very handy man to have around and you could pay him in money or beer, he'd accept either.

When work at the battery ran out I would do a bit of prospecting myself, Ted often came out with me and gave me a hand. He was a very reliable man except when he went on a binge. His binges lasted for two or three weeks and you had to allow him that time, after that he'd be as right as rain again.

I was very fortunate to have my Miner's Rights then because most blackfellas couldn't get it.

It was very hard for people to get the full price for any gold they found, this was especially true for tribal people, who were often paid in tea, sugar or tobacco, and way below what their gold was worth in money terms.

For example, two friends of mine found a big chunk of gold the size of a treacle tin. They took it to a fella called Billy Graham to see how much it was worth.

'Gold eh?', he said when they showed it to him. 'Big fella too. You better let me have a close look at it.'

They handed it to him and he said, 'Mmmmn, it's a big fella all right, but hollow fella too. See all these little pits, white ants bin eatin' him. Rotten, no good, look at the pits!'

They looked at the pits, yes, they could see them.

'Pity about the white ants', he said, 'but seeing as you went to all the trouble of finding it, I'll tell you what I'll do. I'll give you ten bob for it, that means I'm losing five bob myself!'

The silly buggers sold it, they thought Billy was doing them a good turn. There was a big stir about what happened, but no one could do anything because, though Billy had lied, the owners had sold willingly. Sad to say, it wasn't often that the full price was paid to blackfellas.

Billy had a camp just down near the battery, I remember one morning when Scotty and I were working away and we saw Jacky Aspro walk past. He was called that because each time someone asked how he was he'd say he had a headache and ask for an Aspro.

Jacky had been out prospecting and Billy knew. When Jacky walked past he called out, 'Hey Jacky, you got 'em gold?'

'No, I got no gold.'

'Course you have, give it to me.'

'I got no gold.'

'Jacky Aspro if you don't give me that gold I'll shoot you!'

Billy reached behind and pulled out his shotgun. Jacky took off. Billy fired a shot in the air after him. BANG! Jacky shot past us.

'He must be doing ninety-five miles an hour', said Scotty.

'I'd run faster if I had a gun behind me!', I said. BANG! Billy fired another shot that kept Jacky going all the way into Nullagine. We heard later that he sold his gold in there and got a fair price for it. Probably spent the lot on Aspros.

I continued to work at the battery on a regular on-off basis. During that time I paid off all my debts and saved enough money to buy a car, it was a Maxwell Chrysler, and we had a lot of fun in it. It meant I could drive the family around and take them on picnics and so on.

Susie was pregnant again by then with Ronnie, our fourth child, so towards the end of the year I took her into Port Hedland Hospital to have the baby. They were letting a few Aboriginal people in by then. I stayed in Port Hedland for a few months and then returned to Nullagine.

I was happy working at the battery because the people were good and you could depend on the pay. No one tried to rob you. It gave me a feeling of security for the family.

In 1939 a ministerial group from the Labor Party came through Nullagine. They let it be known that they'd be around for a week and would be holding meetings and wanted all the prospectors to come in to them. I decided I might go to the meetings just to see what they had to say. They talked about how they were after better conditions for the working man, they said they wanted to help Aborigines too, let us into schools so the kids could be educated and things like that. I have to admit I was impressed with what they said, I felt they were for the working man so I decided to join the Labor Party, I've been a member ever since.

Bill Hegney got in as Member for the North that year as there was an election on. He was a Labor man so I hoped some good would come from it.

When war was declared there were a lot of fund-raising activities that went on around the area, raising money for the Red Cross and all that sort of thing. I had tried to join up but they wouldn't take me because I only had one good eye, so I tried to support the fund-raising as much as I could. Susie and I went along to all the picnics and dances and tried to help out in any way we could.

There were some very good white people in Nullagine at that time and they didn't draw a distinction with us being Aboriginal or anything like that. They classed us like them, they didn't class us as bush blackfellas.

It was a good time for me and I enjoyed it, but I still felt torn between the white people and the Mulbas. I knew that if I let on to the white people that my heart was really with the Mulbas, I'd be falling out with them. It was very hard then to be a blackman and a whiteman. It seemed that you had to choose one way or the other, no one would let you be both. The problem was, if you chose to be a Mulba you and your family never had any rights at all and you could kiss any hopes of getting on goodbye. Yet if you chose to be a whiteman, you had rights, but you couldn't mix with everyone. It was very hard, very hard.

Later during that year I traded in my Chrysler for a ute because I thought it would be more practical. It was, but not in the way I intended. It meant I often had a ute full of drunks to deliver home. I wasn't into heavy drinking then, but nearly everyone else I knew was. I'd drive into Nullagine and they'd all be lying around the place calling for a lift home. I could never refuse. Ted was one of the ones I often gave a lift to, and he'd make sure everyone else piled in as well, he was very generous like that.

I remember one night they all climbed in the back and I took off on the usual run, I was heading back to my own camp at the twenty-mile and I normally dropped all the others off at different stops along the way. My mate Ted Greig was lying on top of everyone else this particular night, still drinking from his bottle.

What I didn't know was that Jack Parkes, the bloke who'd shot Bobby years before on a droving trip, after Bobby had bested him in a fight, was also in the back. Somehow he'd been thrown on with the rest of them, because he was working in the area at the time.

Anyway, I heard this fella say to Ted, 'Give us a drink!'

'Who are you?', asked Ted. He must have had a real good look at him because the next thing I heard Ted saying was, 'Ooh, I know who you are, you're the mankiller!'

Ted picked up a little stick that was lying on the bottom of the tray and said, 'You mankiller, you killed a blackfella, but you're not killing me. You see this wokkaburra, I'll kill you now if you touch me!'

I peered out the side of the ute window to see if there was going to be trouble, but when I saw the little twig that Ted was holding I just laughed.

We drove out as far as Middle Creek when the mankiller called out, 'Where are we now?'

'Near the Barton turn off,' I yelled.

'Ooh good', Ted called back. 'Let's slide this bastard down that hole at the All Nations mine, that'll save me killing him with this wokkaburra!'

You can imagine that any blackfellas in the back thought this was really funny. Everyone knew what had gone on years before, and they couldn't help laughing at old Wallabong, a whiteman, deciding it was time someone got revenge.

We finally reached the mankiller's camp and Ted sang out, 'If he can't get out, I'll kick him out! I'll drag him out and I'll hit him with this wokkaburra!' He was still hanging onto that little bit of rotten stick.

Luckily, the mankiller managed to roll himself off the truck and we took off.

'Thank God the stink's gone', Ted called. 'By gee he was lucky I didn't whack him with this wokkaburra!' We were all laughing like buggery by then, Ted just wouldn't shut up, he went on and on.

When I finally got to his camp he said, 'Jack, if you see that bastard still lying on the road on your way back, run over him! If you miss him I'll get him tomorrow with my wokkaburra!'

I think after that night everyone felt that in some way justice had been done. Funnily enough I never ever saw that bloke again, maybe he was afraid of Ted's wokkaburra after all.

By the end of that year, 1939, I finally decided to give up my land. I'd battled and battled with it, but nature had finally beaten me. It was very hard to let go my dream of having a station of my own. I had to choose between spending money on the station or my family. It might have been different if there was only me and Susie, but I had to think of the children, they were always needing something and they would have had to go without even more if I hung onto the land.

There was no school in Nullagine in those days and people began pressuring me to get my kids educated. Marie and Johnny were coming up to school age and I wasn't sure what I was going to do about them. I knew I didn't want them to learn to read off jam tin labels the way I'd had to. I wanted something better for them. People kept saying to me, 'You've got your Exemption, that means your kids have to go to school'.

At that time the school in Marble Bar wasn't open either. It had been closed in the 1920s because there weren't enough white kids to keep it open. Marble Bar had become nearly a ghost town in the 1920s. White people around the area then mainly sent their kids to boarding school so I thought perhaps I should do the same thing.

I had no one to give me advice so I ended up writing to Neville and telling him that I was anxious for my children to get an education, and could he recommend anywhere I could send them.

It was early 1940 by the time he replied. He said he had looked into the matter and had decided it wasn't appropriate to send them to Moore River as I was exempted. I breathed a sigh of relief when I read that. I didn't want my kids going there, and it never even occurred to me that that might happen. He said he had talked with the Salvation Army and they had agreed to take the children and educate them for a cost of eight shillings per week per child.

I knew it was going to be hard for me to raise that money on a regular basis. I didn't know what was the right thing to do. I talked it over with Susie and she was more concerned with the kids staying with us than with them being educated. She'd always been a good mother, no one could fault her on the way she looked after the kids. We didn't seem to be able to come to any agreement on what was the right thing, so in the end I decided to leave it a bit longer and see if there was any other way.

Around that time the Comet mine was hiring men so I thought that if I could get a job there, I could move in to the Bar and there might be someone there who I could pay to teach the kids because there wasn't anyone around Nullagine. I drove up to the Comet one week and approached the manager about a job.

'I can't hire you', he said, 'if I hire you all the white blokes will walk off, they won't stand for it'.

'But I've got my Exemption', I said, 'I've been living up to the whiteman's standard, why can't you hire me. I know you need men.'

'That Exemption Certificate won't make any difference to them, as far as they're concerned you're still a nigger. I'm sorry, it's nothing personal, but there's no chance at all of you getting work here.'

I returned to Nullagine very disappointed. Sometimes my Exemption wasn't worth the paper it was written on. There was very little work at the battery then, so I got a job with Billy Mackinnon. He was a nice old fella, a prospector. That poor bugger didn't have much either, but whatever we got out of the ground we shared equally.

I worked with him for about six weeks when one day Claude Martin, the Roads Board's President, came through. He'd often

139

talked to me about sending the kids to school and this time he approached me about it again.

'Look Jack', he said, 'the school is going to open in the Bar soon and there's a possibility that the nightman's job is coming up'.

There was no sewerage in those days so you had to empty the pans by hand at night.

'Oh yes', I said, 'and how does that help me?'

'Well, why don't you move into the Bar. If the nightman's job comes up I'll make sure you get it. If it doesn't, I'm sure there'll be some kind of work for you with the Roads Board.'

I thought it over and decided it was worth the risk. Susie was keen on the idea because it meant the children didn't have to leave home. Also, I figured if worse came to worst I could always move back to Nullagine. We ended up leaving and moving in to Marble Bar in 1941.

12
A Feeling Of Security
1941-1944

When we moved into the Bar the nightman's job wasn't available so I decided to have another go at the Comet, but they told me they still weren't hiring any Aboriginal men.

Fortunately, the Roads Board offered me a job doing pick and shovel work. It wasn't easy work like it is these days. Our front-end loader then was a shovel, our tip truck was a wheelbarrow and all us poor blokes were the bloody engine. It was very hard work, but at least the pay was regular and that counted for a lot then.

I knew that now I was living right in a town I had to be careful to behave like a whiteman. I couldn't just camp anywhere. I made a temporary camp for us on a friend's property near the river, but I knew it was only temporary and I would have to find something better.

Don Thompson, the Secretary of the Roads Board, suggested to me that I take up some land myself. 'No one can move you off your own block Jack', he said, 'I advise you to go and see the Clerk of Courts and tell him you're working for us and that you want to lease some land the proper way'.

I thought this was good advice so I went to see the Clerk of Courts.

'I think that'll be all right', he said, 'there's a bit of land you can take up just out of town, but you'd better check with Gordon Marshall first to make sure it's all right'. Gordon Marshall was the policeman.

I went and saw him and he said, 'Well, it sounds all right to me, but have you seen the Clerk of Courts?'

'Yes, he said it was all right but I had to check with you first.'

'I don't see any problem as long as you continue to live like a whiteman. I'll back you up if there's trouble.'

So that was how I eventually got my block.

I scrounged around after that for material to make a shelter with. There was a shortage of material then because of the war, but I managed to find enough bits and pieces to build one large room. I cut wood for the main posts from down near the river, and someone donated some tin for my roof and things like that. No one complained about my building, so I suppose it wasn't too bad. Also, everyone around knew I belonged to the area so it wasn't as if I was a stranger moving in.

When the school finally opened, there was still a bit of a colour bar but I managed to get my children in. At that time they wouldn't just accept any kid, you had to prove yourself a bit first. Things didn't really open up at the school until 1944, there were all colours going there then. Up until that time Aboriginal people didn't try too much to get their kids in because they knew they'd be rejected.

The other good thing about being in the Bar was my Aunty Dinah, it meant I could see a lot of her because she was working part-time at the hospital there. Whenever I could over the years, I had kept in contact with her, she'd been a mother to me and that was how I thought of her.

I was a bit worried about her because she didn't seem too well to me and I knew her legs were giving her trouble. I persuaded her to give up work and come and live with us for a while.

She stayed with us for three weeks but then decided she wanted to move out and camp in the Moolyella area, it was her favorite place and about twelve miles from the Bar. I drove her out there. There were others camped there so I knew she'd be all right and it wasn't so far out that I couldn't keep an eye on her. She'd developed a bad cold by then and I told her I'd bring her out some medicine as soon as I could.

I bought some Buckley's Cough Mixture, but wasn't able to take it out till the following night.

Paddy Darby saw me pull in and came out and said, 'We lost

your mother this morning Jack, we've already buried her'.

There was no such thing as holding the body in those days, you were buried as soon as possible. I was very upset about losing her so suddenly, she really was my dear old mother.

The following Sunday I drove out and put a marker on her grave. Clancy was out on the station when she died and Jack was still in Perth. I made sure they got word that Dinah was gone.

In 1942 my daughter Doreen was born. They'd brought in Child Endowment by then so I applied for it, but they granted it only after they checked that I was still living up to the whiteman's standard.

I was working pick and shovel one day when one of the other blokes said, 'Did you know there was underground contract work going at the Comet. Supposed to be good money too.'

'No good to me, they've already knocked me back twice. Won't have Aboriginal people.'

'Oh yeah? Then how come an Aboriginal mate of yours has just started there?'

'That's news to me.'

'It's wartime mate, not enough blokes to go around, why don't you give it another go, I'm going to.'

I decided they could only say no again, and all I'd be losing was a bit more pride.

I went to see Don Thompson first. 'I hear the Comet is paying very good money for underground work, would you mind if I applied?'

'If you think you can better yourself Jack, go ahead. But remember, as long as I'm Secretary there's always a job for you here.'

I went and saw the manager, it was the same bloke who'd knocked me back twice before.

'Have you done much shovel work?', he asked.

'I've been hanging on the end of a shovel for years', I told him.

'Okay, when can you start?'

'Well, I'll have to hand in my notice and find a house out this way for the family first.'

'There's an empty one near Mackinnon's mine. You could have that if you like.'

I couldn't believe my ears, it was all so easy, too easy. Why couldn't it have been like that years before?

I took the job and within four days we'd moved into our new home and I was working underground, trucking.

Trucking was hard work but you could make it harder than it was. We had a rake of nine trucks which ran on tram lines underground. My job was more organising than bogging.

The trucks were bogged by what we called a chinaman, which is a grizzly with a shute in the top.

The grizzly is really a grid or a grill made from bars of iron, one to one and a half inches apart. Its overall size is large enough to back a truck into and tip the dirt out. The grid catches all the big stuff but allows the finer stuff through for crushing. The dirt comes down the shute and onto a wooden platform with a trapdoor in it. You position the trucks in turn underneath and when you've got it right you open the trapdoor and let the truck fill up. Then you push it out onto the plat, which is a platform near the main shaft where a cage run on cables is sent down to collect the full truck. You push the truck into the waiting cage and then ring the bell to let upstairs know it's ready to go. They return the cage with an empty truck and so on.

Sometimes there was a plat-man to help you, you only had to fill the trucks and he would do the rest. If there were no plat-men your pay was a bit higher because you had to fill and plat your own dirt. On contract I was being paid five bob a truck and in one day I did seventy-four trucks. That's a record that's never been beaten.

Over the years there's been a lot of money made from the Comet, it's been a very successful mine. It's a pity that all of the money has gone to whitemen.

In the early days white prospectors couldn't work out where the gold was coming from. They searched high and low but couldn't figure it out. Part of the problem was that the rocks around there just didn't look like gold bearing rocks, and yet gold kept turning up.

Anyway, Old Ginger, who was a relation of mine, he belonged to that area and he often collected gold and sold it in town. One day a prospector said, 'Ginger, you show us where you get your gold from and we'll give you something good'. Ginger took them and showed them some green rocks on the top of the hill and they figured it out from there. That green rock is like a sulphide, it goes fifteen ounces to the ton when crushed, but you can't see a speck of gold in that rock with the naked eye, because it's all covered over with other minerals. And what did Ginger get for his troubles? One bag of flour, that's all.

A lot of mineral exploration has been conducted like that in this country. You read in the history books about all the pioneers discovering this and that, somebody should ask them what blackfellas they talked to first.

I don't think the Comet hired me simply because there was a shortage of men. There were other things happening then that began to slowly change people's attitudes. The Labor Party was making a contribution, they had been pressuring businesses for some time to hire more Aboriginal people.

Also, I noticed that with black and white working together at the Comet people started to mix up more and be less suspicious of one another.

I was pleased to have the Comet job, and to be earning what I considered really good money. It was the flushest I'd been in my life and it gave me a feeling of security. The other surprise I had then, besides actually getting the job, was meeting up with Harry Farber again. He had four kids by then and was working for the Comet carting water. He still had his old Cobb and Co. coach that we had used as a tucker cart and one old mule who I recognised as old Lincon. It turned out his house was only three-quarters of a mile away from mine.

We began to talk and had plenty of beers together. We became good friends. He was an entirely different man by then, his attitude towards Aboriginal people had changed completely.

I remember one time when his son Johnny and my son Johnny were waiting for the school bus together. Somehow they got into a fight and were really getting stuck into one another. Harry ran over, and separated them.

'Now listen you boys', he said, 'your father and I carried on like that in the early days, we don't want our kids doing it too!' That meant a lot to me.

While I was at the Comet I got interested in joining the VDC, the Voluntary Defence Corps. You had to be recommended before

145

you could join and of the twenty of us in the Bar I was the only Aboriginal man, though I think in Port Hedland a few more Aborigines belonged to it.

Every Sunday we'd get rigged up in our packs and uniforms and rifles and walk the four miles to Chinaman's Pool. Just around the bend in the hill there'd be another mob waiting to ambush us, often it was the police, and we had to pretend they were the Japanese. We'd all skirt around and shoot in the air and so on, it was live ammo we were using so you had to be careful.

When we'd got the Japanese to surrender the sergeant would pull out his revolver, line us up and put us through exercises. BANG!, he'd shoot and we'd be off, running over rocks and hills, sweating like pigs, pretending to shoot and then hide from the enemy. It was great fun.

There was a big fear then that the Japanese would invade Australia through the north because of our unprotected coastline. I think they could have done it because we were not much of a northern defence. No tribal people were allowed in the VDC, I think the government was afraid they might go over to the enemy. There were some very good trackers amongst those people.

To tell you the truth, we often all talked amongst ourselves about the Japanese. Over the years there'd been good relationships between the Aboriginal people and the Afghans and Chinese, so we wondered if the Japanese would be as easy to get on with. Some of the tribal people thought that everyone from that part of the world was the same, so they thought the Japanese would be as good to them as what the Chinese had been. Either way, they figured the Japanese wouldn't be as bad as the Aussies.

I think we came very close to being invaded. Port Hedland was bombed at Twelve Mile Camp. I remember every afternoon, when I was going on shift at the Comet, seeing all the bombers flying out from the secret airbase at Corunna Downs. We counted fifty-two at one time. Sometimes you'd see them coming back after a mission crippled with bits of wings hanging off and things like that. They seemed to manage to get home all right, although I think they did lose one or two.

There are quite a few small caves around Corunna Downs, they're not large enough to be able to stand up in, but they're good for hiding petrol, tyres and ammunition. You wouldn't see anything from the air because all the entrances were covered with bush.

Quite a few Aboriginal people from the Port Hedland area joined up during the war. Arnold, Manny, Bert and Eric Lockyer, Jimmy Clark and Tommy Murphy. Eric and Arnold were killed, but I think all the others came back. I know some of them still wear their medals and march on Anzac Day.

13

Fighting The Department
1944-1946

I continued to work happily at the Comet for twelve months, it was good regular work and I felt I was getting somewhere at last.

Around that time, however, I started to have trouble with my gums. Whenever I bit on anything they hurt. I went and saw Dr Dix and he told me that I had pyorrhoea and would have to go to Perth for treatment.

'There's nothing I can do for you, Jack', he said, 'you'll have to have all your teeth out so you'll need a dentist and you'll have to have a doctor in attendance too because of the infection. I'll give you a letter and you need to get down there as soon as possible.'

It was 1944 then, my last child, Willie, had been born and Susie had just applied for her Exemption and been granted it. Things were looking good for us, except for my bloody gums. I have to tell you I felt very depressed about it. I didn't want to leave my job at the Comet and I didn't want to have to let go of my land. I decided that I was being silly trying to hang on to the land because I didn't know how long I would be away and I would still have to pay rent on it. In the end I sold the lease to Sandy Thompson, Don's brother, because I knew I would need cash to tide the family over in Perth until I could get work.

I told my boss at the Comet that I had to leave and he said, 'I know you're unhappy about it Jack, but it's something you can't avoid, if you don't get it fixed up you might be in worse trouble'.

I was just miserable about the whole thing. I remember sitting in front of the pub that night in Marble Bar, I was a bit under the weather and feeling sorry for myself. Gordon Marshall, the policeman, came up to me and said, 'What's up Jack?' I told him my situation and how I had to leave to go to Perth.

'That's bad luck', he said, 'I hope it all works out for you, when are you going?'

'Next week, Wally Marshall is giving us a lift down on his truck.'

'Well, I think you'll be all right Jack, nothing's beaten you yet. We'll see you back here one day soon.'

He left and I sat there and continued to feel awful. I wasn't worried about losing all my teeth, I was worried about how I was going to support the family, how to get enough money together to come back North, and whether the Aborigines Department would give us a hard time while I was there. It seemed to me that it was easier to live your life if you were a long way from them. Their head office was in Perth and we'd be right under their bloody noses.

We left the following week and arrived in Perth a few days later. I had a relation of mine staying in Fremantle, she'd been taken away from the Bar as a young girl, but we'd managed to keep in touch with one another. Her name was Nellie Barker, but people knew her as Mrs Tressider because she was married to a whitefella who was in the army. She'd said we could stay with her.

After getting lost a few times, Wally finally found her house in Hardy Street, Fremantle. I unloaded Susie and the six kids and we all went inside. It wasn't a bad house, it was a four-room weatherboard place on a hill. I thought the house was good, but there were already a lot of people staying there, Archie Todd, Florrie Walker, Gloria Fitzgerald and my old brother Jack Doherty and his wife Jean and their two kids.

I was really pleased to see Jack again, but I knew that if the Aborigines Department checked the place there'd be trouble.

After we'd settled in I went and saw Dr Hogan and Mr Bennett the dentist. They put me into hospital and took out all my teeth bar four wisdom teeth. I was bleeding a lot and they decided it wasn't safe to remove all of them at once. They told me they'd lost a chap like that only a few months before.

I was sent home for a week and then put into hospital again so they could take out the remaining ones.

149

Unfortunately, while I was in hospital the Aborigines Department got onto us.

Nellie had told me the week before that I wasn't to worry about Neville because he'd left around 1940, which was about the last time I had written to him.

I remember saying to her, 'Are you sure?' It seemed too good to be true that the bastard had finally gone of his own accord, in my mind, no one could be worse than him. It was because he had left that I went into hospital the second time feeling quite light-hearted and thinking that maybe things would change for the better for Mulbas after all.

However, when I came home Susie and Jean told me a different story. A representative of the Department had been and inspected the house. They'd counted the beds and said there weren't enough and that we shouldn't be sleeping on the floor. They told Susie and Jean that some of the people they were living with were natives, including Nellie, who although married to a whiteman didn't have her Exemption. They said that the conditions we were living in were as bad as if we were camp natives and that if we continued to live like that we'd all lose our Exemptions.

I felt really depressed when they told me all of this. Also, with all my teeth now gone I felt bloody awkward, I didn't feel like smiling or talking, it was embarrassing. I decided to try and get a job as soon as possible and then I might be able to rent another house for us. I talked to Archie Todd and George Howard and we all decided to go to Parliament House and see Bill Hegney, who was still Minister for the North, and see if he could give us some advice about how to find work in Perth.

We knocked on the door of Parliament House and had to stop ourselves from laughing when a bloke answered all dolled up in brass buttons and goodness knows what else. I was the only one in control of myself.

'We'd like to see Bill Hegney please', I said.

'Certainly gentlemen, please follow me.' We followed him down the corridor, and all the time were were looking at each other thinking, thank God we didn't have his job.

Bill was in his office and we went straight in and told him our situation.

'If you want work', he told us, 'the best place is to go down to the labour bureau in Milligan Street. You should be able to get work from there, if you can't, come back and see me again.'

We went straight there and found there were two businesses wanting men, Gadsen's Tin Factory and the Colonial Sugar Refinery. They advised us to try the CSR because it was better money.

George decided to look around for something else but Archie and I were desperate so we went down to the CSR and they hired us straight away. We started work there the following morning.

I worked with six other men, and we had to fill a quota of thirty-two bags of molasses for each day. By the end of our shift we looked and tasted like molasses. It was awful. We had to stand under a shower, clothes and all, to get ourselves clean before we could go home. It was very sticky work.

I was doing my best to live a quiet life and ignore the Aborigines Department when they started bothering us again. I went to see my boss at the CSR and told him what was happening.

'We don't want to lose you Jack', he said, 'you're one of our best workers. I'll ring them and see what I can do.'

He rang and asked for a Mr Proud.

'This man's got six children, the father's one of my best workers and you know there's a shortage of rental accommodation in Perth. Why can't he stay where he is, you're making it very difficult for him.' Proud put up a real battle, it seemed he wanted us out of Nellie's house and that was that.

The pressure was really on then. When I wasn't working I was combing Perth trying to find a house to rent. The final straw came when the Fremantle police visited us one night and gave me twenty-four hours to leave. I went and saw my boss and he rang Proud again. All that that achieved was to get our eviction notice extended from twenty-four hours to one week. We were told that if we hadn't left by then the police would come back and evict us.

That was enough for Archie Todd, he was fed up with all the pressure from the Department. He handed in his resignation and headed back North. Jack and Jean hunted around and found a little place out at Gosnells and they moved out there. I couldn't find anywhere to go so in the end the only choice I was left with was moving in with Jack and Jean. I thought that seeing they were exempted, the Department would approve.

Even though we were now a long way from Fremantle I decided to try and keep my job at the CSR. I needed the money to support the family and if I left I didn't know where else I would get a job.

It meant getting up very early to catch the train and home very late. Sometimes the trains weren't on time, so I was late for work and often had my pay docked. It wasn't very satisfactory at all, but I put up with it for four months and then decided to go and see Proud myself. I was hoping I could persuade him to let us move back in with Nellie. I had been keeping my eye out for a house closer to Fremantle, but none had come up.

When I went and saw Proud he said, 'Look, you know the Department's views. They haven't changed. The way I see it you have two alternatives, go back to Marble Bar or try and get some work at the fertiliser factory in Gosnells.'

I didn't have enough money to get the family back to the Bar.

'I've got some mining experience', I told him, 'can you suggest anything in that line?'

'Well, you can try the Hill 50. They have an office here in Perth and a mine in Mt Magnet, they're often looking for men, I'll give you their address.'

'Good, I'll try that.'

'Just remember Jack, there's no chance of any change of mind about you living with Nellie. Also, I've had a report that you're living with the Dohertys and I can't say we're really happy about that either.'

I left then. It seemed it didn't matter what I did I couldn't win, nothing was good enough for the Aborigines Department.

I went straight to Hill 50's main office. I decided then to accept whatever they offered me, just so I could get away from Perth and all the interference. I told them what kind of work I was experienced in and to my relief they hired me straight away to do exactly the same thing at Magnet.

When I got home I talked it over with Susie and we agreed that I would go up first and try to organise a house for the family before they moved up too.

It was 1945 then, and when I arrived in Magnet the policeman came and saw me. Probably Proud had let him know I was coming, I don't know. Anyway, I told him what job I had and asked him if he knew of any houses to rent. He was a nice chap and rented me a house himself. It belonged to someone who was away at war and he was in charge of it.

I started work at the mine straight away and to my surprise I met up with a couple of blokes that I had worked with on Austin Downs years before. They were wonderful men, but we got into having drinking parties together, which probably wasn't a good idea because I hadn't been a heavy drinker up until then.

Leo, Theo, Billy and Wally were hard workers and hard drinkers. Leo lived in a tent about four miles out of town and he loved throwing parties. He'd give you a big feed of bacon first and then he'd plonk a bottle in front of each one of us and we were supposed to knock it off as quick as we could. It was a kind of game.

He always had a big cask full of grog sitting there as well. He'd put a big enamel dish underneath it and fill it up, then he'd get down on his hands and knees and drink it all. We'd all be pretty silly by then so we'd say, 'Oooh, we can do that!' So we'd all be down on our hands and knees lapping up this grog and laughing ourselves silly. I really wonder now how I used to get home.

I'd feel really sick the following morning, I'd make myself drink a big mug of rainwater in the hope that it would make me feel better, but it never did.

It was four weeks before Susie and the kids came up and when she found out about my drinking she was furious. She used to belt me and called me terrible names. Tell me I was a drunken bastard and all that business. I took it all because I knew she was right. And she was such a high-spirited woman I didn't like to disagree with her too much.

She could certainly pack a punch when she wanted to! I thought about giving up the drinking, but it would have meant giving up my friends as well and I found I enjoyed and needed their company. I tried cutting down a bit, but they always forced me to drink more or made me feel I wasn't one of them if I didn't drink the same amount. Looking back now I was bloody silly, but that's how it was in those days. One thing though, I always made sure the drinking didn't interfere with my work. I was never drunk on the job.

After a while Susie made friends with some other women and they were drinkers too. She found then that it was hard to hold out against their pressure. She began to drink a lot more than normal, but still not as much as me. I was the worst. She never let her drinking interfere with her cooking or the kids going to school or anything like that.

While I was at the Hill 50 I had two near fatal accidents. I was near the end of my shift when the boss asked me and another fella to crawl down into a condemned shaft and pick up a universal bar that someone had left there when the shaft was last in use.

The shaft led down into a space that was big enough to fit a house in, it was three hundred foot underground and the guts of it had been mined out so it wasn't in use anymore.

We crawled down slowly hanging onto the rope as we went. It was hard going because the rubble under our feet kept giving away and making us slide a little bit.

We finally got the universal bar and started to head back up. About halfway up we started to hear rumbling and we knew what that meant, we couldn't get up that rope quick enough. Just as we reached the top over one hundred ton of earth crashed down into that space. There would have been only a few seconds between us and instant death. We were very lucky. I've been very, very lucky with death in my life.

The second accident could have been fatal too but luckily it wasn't. A big boulder came flying down the chute one day, it was completely unexpected. There was nowhere for me to run because I was surrounded by big rocks. I dodged it best I could but it still put me in hospital for a week. I was very badly bruised down one side of my body, but that was better than a smashed head. There was no compo in those days but the mine paid my hospital bill, so I didn't have to worry about that.

I hadn't been back at work long when peace was declared. Everyone went mad. We all knocked off work, church bells were ringing, people were throwing their hats and everything in the air. By the end of the day there were drunks everywhere. Everyone was so glad it was over.

Not long after that my friend Jimmy Green had a word to me about citizenship.

'We got to get a dog's licence to walk on the road now Jack', he said.

'What are you talking about?' I asked.

'Nothing we can do about it Jack', he said, 'they want to license us'.

'Who do?'

'The government. They bringing in something called Citizenship for us Aboriginal people, they going to license us.'

'So what else is new?'

'This is serious Jack. There's talk that unless you got it, you won't be able to do much.'

It was all news to me. I had a talk with some of my white mates and they'd heard of it too. They told me I should go for it. They said, 'Look Jack, we know it's not a nice thing to have, but you got a wife and kids to support, it might be something that affects your job. You don't want to be put out of action here, so you should play it safe and go for the bloody thing.'

I talked it over with Susie and we both decided to go for it, but not in Mt Magnet. We decided to try and cut down on our drinking so we could save as much as we could to buy a truck. Then we'd go back to the Bar. Everyone knew us there, it might make it easier. I worked at Hill 50 for another eight months, bought a Dodge truck, and in 1946 we returned to Marble Bar.

14
I'm A Whiteman Now!
1946-1951

We settled back into the Bar, it was good to be home again and to be close to my family and friends. I went down to the Comet and fortunately for me they were shorthanded so I got my job back straight away.

I still felt uneasy about the Citizenship thing, I was worried that they might not approve of us. I knew we both had our Exemptions so I was hoping that might help.

Gordon Marshall was still the policeman there and he helped me fill out the forms and recommended us as being proper people. We had to be examined by a doctor who swore we were free of certain diseases, like leprosy and diphtheria. There were the same conditions about not mixing with Aborigines or supplying them with grog. It was also like the Exemption Certificate in that if you didn't live up to your side of the bargain, you could lose it.

It had never occurred to me before that I might not be an Australian citizen. I thought everyone born here was Australian. My mother had been here before any white people, so I'd never thought we might be considered strangers in our own country. Gordon explained to me that unless you got this new Citizenship you weren't really an Australian at all.

'Well what are you then?', I asked him.

'I dunno.'

'Are you as good as a migrant?'

'Not really, because migrants become citizens.'

'So a Mulba who doesn't go for this is nothing then?'

156

'Well yes, I suppose in the eyes of the law he is nothing.'

It all seemed bloody silly to me, it made you wonder what kind of people were running the country.

Anyway, our applications were sent to Perth. They were signed there and then returned to Marble Bar. A time was arranged for Susie and I to go before a magistrate so he could decide whether we could have it or not.

In the meantime I had to organise witnesses who would stand up for us in court and say that they should grant our application because we were living up to the whiteman's standard.

We were very nervous the day we went to court. Even though we felt we had a good chance because of our Exemption Certificates we were still scared they might not grant us Citizenship. I wore my best clothes and so did Susie and we tried to speak in the proper way and so on.

The magistrate asked my name and where I was working. He had it all on the form in front of him but he asked anyway. Then he said, 'Do you live like white people, you and your wife?'

'Yes sir.'

'Do you get drunk?'

'I have done one or two times with my friends.'

'Will you supply liquor to natives if you're granted this?'

'No sir.'

'Describe to me how you live.'

I did that and then he said, 'Well, you seem all right to me, I think we'll pass you'.

And that was that.

We used to joke about the whole thing amongst ourselves, we could see it was silly, but not many other people thought so. We'd say things to each other like, 'You eating with a knife and fork, is your plate china and not enamel, you better get it right or they might take your Citizenship away!'

Others would say, 'Hey Jack, why do you need that Dog Licence? You walk on two legs not four!' And so it went on, we all called our papers a Dog Licence, we thought that was a better name for it than Citizenship.

I remember when a friend of mine got his papers. He was a bit of a character and he came running down the main street

Jack McPhee, Citizenship photograph, 1946.

of Marble Bar from the courthouse shouting, 'I'm a whiteman, I'm a whiteman, I just left my black skin at the courthouse!' By gee, he was funny, I laughed and laughed.

Then he said to me, 'Hullo whitefella, you got your whiteskin on?'

'Ooh yes', I said, 'can't you see I've changed colour?'

'Courthouse got your old skin too eh? I hope you've got a silver knife, no more tin for you. No more enamel mugs, we got to have bone china now.'

By gee he was silly, he made a big joke of the whole thing and I really enjoyed it.

Of course there was a lot of conflict between those who had their Citizenship and those who didn't. Some people who could have gone for it refused to on principle; ngayarda banujuthas never went for it because they knew they wouldn't get it and felt it was of little use anyway. Those of us who went for it were hoping for something better for ourselves and our families, that was our main reason. The Mulbas who decided against it thought we were too flash for them. They thought we were putting ourselves above our own people. They were real sarcastic buggers. You'd walk down the street and they'd call out, 'Hey whitefella!', or, 'Don't get too close whitefella, our black might rub off on you!' And they were your friends!

There was a big problem with the grog too. We used to come under all kinds of pressure to buy grog, it was terrible. Mulbas are very good at making you feel awful, especially when they're related to you. You had to be really strong to hold out because supplying liquor was a very serious offence and a very quick way to lose your Citizenship. I was caught this way once myself.

It was Christmas time and Dougall came up to see me. He was loaded up with goodies for his family, and he said, 'Look Jack, you can see how loaded up I am, I can't manage a case of wine as well, here's the money, can you buy one for me and I'll pick it up later on. Take a bottle out for yourself as well.'

He was that casual about it that I assumed he had his rights. I took the money and bought the wine and Dougall picked it up late in the afternoon.

The next day Gordon Marshall came down and asked me if

I'd bought wine for Dougall. I told him I had, that I'd taken one bottle for myself and that Dougall had taken the rest home.

'Never mind about home, Jack', said Gordon, 'he took the case down to the reserve, they all got drunk and had a hell of a big fight down there. The gaol's nearly full! Did you know Dougall hasn't got any rights?'

'No, I thought he had them.'

'This is serious Jack, you know how the Aborigines Department feels about this sort of thing.'

'Well he was that casual about it I just thought he must have rights.'

'You better not do any more assuming, make sure first. I'll put in a good word for you because I wouldn't like to see you lose your rights, but I can't promise anything. The judge will have to decide when you go to court.'

'I'd appreciate that, thank you.'

'Look Jack, I know it's hard for you, but I have to give you a warning about something else as well. I can't help noticing that you've always got a few natives and half-castes round your place. I know they haven't got any rights and you're supposed to be living like a whiteman and not mixing with them. Now, it's my job to keep an eye out for these things and to report to the Aborigines Department, I can't keep turning a blind eye. I have to tell you that by consorting with natives you're in danger of losing your Citizenship. I've warned you, so it's up to you what you do about it.'

What was I supposed to do? They were my friends and relations. Mulbas aren't like white people when it comes to their relations, it's very hard to cut them off. You always have obligations to relations, even if you don't like them. None of them were troublemakers, we just enjoyed mixing up together.

I went to court not long after and breathed a sigh of relief when I was only fined twenty quid. That was the only time I was ever caught for supplying liquor, there were other times when I gave my mates a drink, but I made sure everyone kept it quiet so there was no trouble.

About a month after I'd been to court Gordon Marshall got a letter from the Aborigines Department saying that they'd noticed that I had been convicted for supplying liquor to natives and according to the Natives Citizenship Act of 1944 I could lose my Citizenship on any of three grounds.

'You better listen Jack', Gordon said, 'because these are the grounds. First, if you fail to adopt the manner and habits of civilised life. Second, if you get convicted of the same offence twice or are drunk a lot. Third, if you come down with leprosy, yaws, syphilis or granuloma. Now, I've done my duty and read that to you. Now, they want me to reply saying whether I think they should take your rights away from you or not. I want you to know I'm telling them I don't think it's necessary, but I'm telling you all this so you can see that it's very serious and so you'll be careful about the way you live in the future.'

I thanked him for supporting me. I knew it was hard for him because he had a job to do and if I wasn't very careful he might not have any choice but to recommend that I lose my rights.

The year that I was granted my Citizenship was the same year of the now famous Pilbara strike by Aboriginal station workers. I was kept well informed about the goings on of the strikers because one of the leaders was Clancy McKenna and he used to tell me what they were fighting for.

Even though Clancy was a mardamarda like me he was one of the ones that didn't agree with either the Exemption or the Citizenship. He was a big, clever man and he could turn his hand to anything. He was also more of a thinker than I was, and he felt a deep responsibility to his mother's people. While I had been mainly brought up by whites, he'd spent more time with blacks. They'd gotten into his head and heart and it was impossible for him to pull away from them. I could understand this and at the same time he could understand me, so even though we had different views, we were still close to one another.

The other difference between me and Clancy was that he was fearless and I wasn't. He faced trouble head on, even encouraged it if he felt it was right. I tried to live a quiet life and avoid fights with the police and the Aborigines Department. I couldn't help admiring Clancy because he was so game. He'd walk into a pub knowing he had no rights and demand a drink. He'd answer squatters back and disagree with their views. He was a fighter.

161

Clancy was very impressed with Don McLeod. He was a whiteman, but he was for the blackman. He helped the strikers to organise themselves, and advised them right through the strike. Don McLeod thought black people should be treated the same as whites, and I think it was he who started Clancy thinking that something could be done, and that you didn't just keep putting up with bad treatment.

I remember Clancy telling me, 'Striking is the only way, we don't want to be treated like dogs anymore. Sour bread and kangaroo, old tea and no pay, it's not right Jack. Now, you take my mob, there were thirty of us working on the station and only three of us getting paid, and then it wasn't much. You see I've found out some things Jack, white people can't kill us these days, that's too much, all they can do is try and frighten us, tell lies about us and put us in gaol. I'm happy to go to gaol for my people. I don't think there's any shame in going to gaol when you're fighting for better conditions.'

It was just as well because Clancy was in and out of gaol all during the strike. I thought that was very unfair. I used to say to him, 'I understand why you're striking and I agree with it. Do you think I don't know what it's like? Why do you think I went for my Exemption and my Citizenship, because I want something better too and that's my way of trying to get it.'

'That's all right for mardamardas', he used to say, 'but no good for the other Mulbas, they got no rights, they got to fight for them. The only thing they got is their labour, the only way the squatters will listen is if we walk off and they left with no labour. They'll be in a mess then.'

I knew Clancy was right. You couldn't reason with squatters. They'd been treating the blackfellas rotten for years, they'd never improved on their treatment at all. Keep them down, work them hard, give them as little as possible, that was their way. In those days a whiteman could earn in one week what a squatter would pay a whole group of blacks. Also, a lot of blacks were the best workers, they were reliable, experienced and honest, but this was never recognised.

I think during the strike over one thousand Mulbas walked off stations in the Pilbara. Some were forced back over the next few years and some went back when they were offered better conditions, but in the end over eight hundred refused to go back at all. They figured any way was better than the old way.

The squatters were dishonest then. They got the Aborigines Department to pressure the strikers, they involved the police, they made all sorts of threats to people. Many I know were gaoled for no good reason or on some charge that someone made up. It was very unfair.

The squatters' argument was that if they were forced to pay equal wages to blacks they'd go broke, but they'd had slave labour for years and years. They'd treated Mulbas like animals, using the women whenever it suited them and working the men for nothing. I knew that what the strikers were saying was true, I knew what it was like and I felt very sympathetic to Clancy and tried to help him with a few bob whenever I could.

That was why, when Don McLeod came and asked me if I knew any good spots for prospecting, I told him to try wolfram. For many years the price had been too low for anyone to bother mining it, but I had a suspicion it had gone up.

Don's mob were desperate for money by then. They needed to be able to feed the women and kids. They had to find some kind of work outside the stations if they wanted to be independent of the squatters. I gave Don the names of two fellas I knew in Nullagine who could point him in the right direction. It turned out that my advice was pretty good. After a lot of hard work they did well out of it. I think they went on to mine antimony too.

Don was all for the blackfellas getting some money together and buying their own station and Clancy was for this too at first, but later on he pulled away from that mob and went out on his own. You see, he felt that while he was pulling his weight and working very hard for the people, there were others that were not doing their fair share. Yet when it came to money and food, they were all treated the same and Clancy felt this was unfair. I know he was disappointed in some of the younger ones who didn't seem to be really interested in taking any responsibility. He felt that he and Peter Coffin and Ernie Mitchell were carrying too much of the burden for everyone else.

I think that's why in the end there was a split with some

blackfellas staying with Don and buying Strelley Station and with others going with Ernie and Peter.

Ernie and Peter went on to establish a place of their own called Yandeearra. Clancy used to go there now and then, he built the big water tank there. Peter was keen for him to stay but he wanted to be on his own by then. I've been out to Yandeearra myself over the years. It's a very good place. Peter runs it real good. They have a school there now and some good houses and Peter makes sure the old people are taken care of.

Clancy was the same as me in that he wanted to own something of his own and he wanted his own efforts recognised. He wasn't keen on this group ownership thing that people seem to talk about now. He reckoned everyone should have the same rights and opportunities, and he shouldn't have to support a blackfella who he thought was lazy if he didn't want to.

Now people have this idea that Mulbas like having joint ownership of land and so on, but Clancy didn't want that. Some Mulbas are like that yes, but many are not. The trouble with that way of looking at things is, as Clancy found, a few end up supporting the many. Also, it's hard to make decisions because while everyone wants to have their say, no one wants to take any responsibility. I don't agree with it at all. I think it's good for a man and his family to own their own place, but once the group starts getting bigger than that you can have troubles.

Now, I wanted my own station and I would have had all my children and friends working for me too, but there would be no arguments about who was the boss or who the station belonged to.

I know it's a good thing for there to be leaders for people, but if everyone gets dependent on one person and won't take any responsibility for their part, when that person goes it makes it very hard. I think it's better if each man can learn to pull his weight, do his bit, take responsibility for himself and his family and then help the others along when he can. That's just how I think of course, but it seems to make sense to me.

Clancy stayed pretty discouraged by everything. Even though good things had come from the strike for others, he still didn't have the right way for himself. I think he felt that now it was

164

all over he wouldn't find it either. He even took to thinking about Citizenship. He was looking for something that would make him completely equal to the whiteman. He made enquiries about it but he just couldn't understand why, if he was born in this country, as was his mother and her mother, he needed it. I think because he couldn't see the reason for it he decided against it. As I said before, Clancy was a thinking man. He wasn't the kind of person to go along with you unless it made real good sense to him.

Anyway, I've gone off the track a bit. Towards the end of 1946 I left the Comet because the work was winding down, I was only doing the odd shift and it wasn't enough money to make it worth my while. I went down and worked at the Blue Speck Mine in Nullagine for a while, as did a lot of other blokes from the Comet.

My job was on the plant. I had to weigh the balls and put them in the mill, which was like a big forty-four gallon drum. I kept a tally of the balls that went in. They were very heavy cast iron, and you had to be accurate about what you were doing. The balls were used to crush the stone to get the gold and antimony out. As the balls crushed the rock in the mill, water would come in and carry the waste away.

While I was at the Blue Speck I had a bad accident. There was a sump on the floor that fed the mill, and the pump on it was run by electricity. There was a belt going from the motor to the centrifugal pump. Sometimes the motor used to jam, the men complained about it often, but we all worked out that if you gave the belt a quick pull the motor would kick over and start working, so that was what we used to do.

One morning I was there I switched the pump on, but the motor failed to kick over. Needs a pull, I thought. What I didn't know then was that the bloke in the main powerhouse hadn't got around to turning the main switch on. He realised his mistake and, unfortunately, turned the switch at the same time as I pulled the belt. Of course the thing started up instantly and I lost the top off my thumb.

They called the Flying Doctor in from Marble Bar and I was very lucky because he managed to save my thumb. It looks a bit funny, but it's still there so I can't complain.

There was still no compo then, and I was off work for six weeks, so I had to use the bit of money that I had saved to keep the family going. I used to book up a lot at the store in the Bar. They didn't mind because they knew me and trusted me to pay when I could.

I went back to the Blue Speck when I was better, but I didn't stay long because the work was cutting out there too. I decided to try prospecting myself in the Moolyella area for tin.

I did that for a few months, but it wasn't enough to keep the wife and kids, so I asked the Roads Board if there was anything going and they gave me a job. It was 1947 by then.

The job with the Roads Board involved lots of different kinds of work. You went wherever you were needed, it could be anything from pick and shovel, to collecting pans, to looking after the town water supply.

Tommy Stream came to us that year and asked us to take in his three children. He was working on Corunna Downs and his wife had died and he had no one to look after them. Normally I don't agree with that sort of thing, but Tommy was a relation and in a real hard spot. We were struggling ourselves trying to feed our own kids, but Susie had always had a soft spot for kids so we ended up taking them in. They were with us for three years and then Tommy took them back when he got another woman.

I continued to work on and off for the Roads Board. When there wasn't any work going around the Bar I'd contract for work on stations or prospect to help make ends meet.

During this time I bumped into two of my best old mates, Wonguynon and Rosie, who'd been on Corunna Downs when I'd been there. They were camped out at Shaw River with some others and had come into the Bar for a visit. I didn't recognise them at first. They were talking away and I was a little bit slow in saying anything because I was trying to work out who they were. Then they started making jokes about Corunna and teasing me and of course I recognised them straight away.

We had a good old talk about the old days then, and I told them what I'd been up to over the years. When Wonguynon heard I'd been in Perth she said, 'Perth? You seen my sister Daisy* or

---

* Daisy Corunna: Sally Morgan's maternal grandmother.

166

my brother Arthur?'

I told her I had looked for them but hadn't been able to find them. Others had mentioned to me that I must look out for them and I had, I'd even asked around to see if anyone knew where they had gone, but they just seem to have disappeared. You have to understand that it's not like it is now with blackfellas all over the place. We all knew each other then and considered ourselves to be countrymen, brothers.

That was the last time I saw those two. They went back to their camp at Shaw River. There were no buildings there or anything, just bough-sheds, but it was a good place for yandying tin and Don Thompson had a store there so they could buy food and any other things they needed.

In 1950 I was still with the Roads Board but it was more of a permanent type of job by then. I looked after the water pump that controlled the town water supply. I'd start the pump in the morning to make sure the water tanks on top of the hill were full. While the pump was working I'd go round and take care of the sanitary, that meant I had to cart the pans away. I usually finished around ten o'clock and would spend the rest of the day checking on the water level on and off. When I saw the tanks were full I'd turn the pump off and wouldn't turn it on again until three o'clock in the afternoon, that was when people started to water their lawns. Then I'd make sure the tanks were full before I knocked off so people had enough water for bathing and cooking.

I worked there regularly for around twelve months until one day, Don Beaton, who was managing Mullyie Station, came in and offered me a job.

'We're very shorthanded Jack', he said, 'you know a lot of those strikers are never coming back, they want to set up on their own now. If you take the job there's a house for you, you'll be earning more than you're getting here. I'll make sure you get your basic rates and your keep won't be any extra. Your older girls can work in the house so they'll have a bit of money too and there's a governess out there, she can see to the kids' schoolwork.'

The more he talked, the better it sounded. I wasn't going anywhere doing what I was doing. And I knew Marie and Josie, who were teenagers then, would like some money.

Jack McPhee with friend, Doris Mitchell, Marble Bar, c.1950.

'It sounds all right to me', I said, 'I'm a bit sick of the sanitary and I've always loved station work. I'll have to give a fortnight's notice though.'

'That's all right. You know any boys who might want a job too?'

'My boy Johnny could do with a bit of work and there's Johnson Taylor, he's a good boy, I think he'd go.'

'Good, I'll take them both. Can they come out before you?'

'Yes, I think they would, I'll have a word to them.'

'Tell you what, I'll send the truck tomorrow to pick up the family, you can come out when you're finished up here.'

I suppose it might seem disloyal for me to work on Mullyie when the strikers wouldn't, but as I said before, I saw my way as being different. They all knew that it was me that had put Don onto the wolfram and because they knew I had my Citizenship they put me in a different class to themselves. I suppose they were trapped in their way and I was trapped in mine and probably neither of us was completely right but you just had to try the best way you could.

I knew Susie would be pleased to go out to Mullyie because she'd always preferred station life to town life. Also, Mullyie was sixty miles north from the Bar so it would get us both away from some of our mates who drank too much. I was still drinking heavily, but not nearly as much as when I was at Hill 50. Susie was drinking too and that worried me a little, but she was good with the meals and the kids so I couldn't say too much. I knew some of her mates talked her into drinking more than she normally would, and I could understand that because I had the same problem myself. Mullyie would be good for all of us.

15

A Working Man
1951-1961

On Mullyie I was put in charge of the mustering camp. My son Johnny was working with me, he was a good boy and loved station work. I think it was in his blood. Don would tell me what he wanted done around the station and I would organise the boys to do it, so I suppose I was like a second manager. Don was good to work for because he trusted you to work on your own.

I'd only been there five weeks when Don was given the sack. I don't know why they sacked him because he was a good man, straight and honest. The governess left the same time as Don and when the new manager, Ben Jones, took over, his wife taught the children their schoolwork. The new manager was good too, and we often talked about the strike together and the conditions on other stations.

Ben told me he was against Mark Reuben for not paying better wages. Reuben owned Mullyie, as well as a number of other stations in the area. I think he'd made his money in pearling in the early days and put it all into stations and real estate. There were hardly any squatters then who gave blacks a fair go.

Ben asked me if I'd like to do some fencing to fill in the gap between mustering and everything else. He said he could get a contractor in, but if I wanted the contract I might as well take it.

He offered me twenty-five quid for every mile fenced.

I said, 'That's not enough Ben, I have to pay out wages myself on it, you know I'll have to hire a bloke to help me. I won't do

170

it under thirty quid a mile.'

'All right, thirty a mile. The station will supply the wire and side posts, but you'll have to cut your own strainers and supply your own food and fuel.' We agreed on that.

A lot of station work was contract work in those days. There was no set price for anything, it was whatever you could negotiate with the boss. Generally you asked for more than what you really wanted to start off with, because it was accepted that the boss would beat you down.

I hired Harry Davis and Archie Ball to give me a hand because they were looking for a bit of extra money themselves.

We had to fence all along the river. That meant digging a posthole every five chains, so every five chains there's a wooden strainer and all the ones in between are wire posts. It was about a month's work and we fenced just over ten miles in that time.

Now, at the same time I was doing that fencing, there was a white bloke on De Grey Station, who had been hired by another of Reuben's managers to do fencing too. I found out later that he had been paid sixty quid a mile, and he didn't have to cut his own strainers. I suppose it was my own fault really because I should have asked for a lot more to begin with. The point I want to make is, in those days, Aboriginal men were always expected to work for less.

When the work began to wind down on Mullyie I decided to bring the family down to Perth for a holiday. There was no point in hanging around doing nothing. With station work, you only got paid till the work cut out, and then you were expected to find something else. So, while you were earning, you had to save money to tide yourself over when you weren't. Anyway, Ben kindly lent me one of the trucks on Mullyie so I could bring the family down to Perth.

We camped in some nice bush just north of Guildford. There was a soak nearby, so water was no problem. After three days of lazing about we all went into Guildford to do some shopping. Johnny and Peter, Marie's boyfriend, were getting pretty bored by then. They wanted something to do, they weren't keen on this holiday business.

While we were in town Rab Bell, who owned Bell Brothers, came

171

up to me.

'That your truck with the Marble Bar numberplate?'

'Yes.'

'Good! Look, I'm shorthanded and I've seen a few of you blokes around town this morning, what about working for me?'

'We're here for a holiday', I told him, 'we've been working hard, we want a bit of a break'.

'It'll only be a few days, I'll pay well.'

'What doing?'

'Clearing land at Kwinana.'

'No, I don't think so.' I wasn't keen to take that on at all. Clearing land can be very hard work. Rab left me and went over to talk to Johnny and Peter. Blow me down if the boys didn't agree to work for him.

'What about your holiday?' I complained to them.

'Weekends are holiday enough', they said, 'we'd rather work than sit around here, and we could do with some money'. They went off with Rab to start work straight away and Susie and I followed two days later. I could have let them do it on their own, but I didn't feel right about it. They were only young, I wanted to make sure I kept an eye on them.

The camping area at Kwinana was good and the kids really loved the beach. However, the bush there was the sort that was very hard to clear. Rab had given us the impression that it would be an easy job, it wasn't at all. There were some huge blackboys there and they can be very hard to get out.

We worked there for a week when Rab came down and said, 'That'll do for now, I want you to come up to Red Hill and do some work up there'. Red Hill was just off the Toodyay road, north of Perth.

'You haven't given us any money for this yet, Rab', I said. He gave me a few quid and the boys a few bob and said he'd pay us the balance when we'd finished at Red Hill. I should have caught on then, but I didn't. I wasn't keen to go to Red Hill but I felt I had to in order to get the money he owed us.

We moved up to Red Hill and while we were there we heard that Rab had been trying to get someone to clear his Kwinana land for a long time, but no one would do it because he refused to pay what it was worth. I was starting to think then we'd been suckered.

We did some fencing on Red Hill and had to cut all our own posts and that sort of thing. We'd been there about five days when Rab came and said, 'I'm not satisfied with the job you're doing'.

He went on and on picking at this and that.

'They don't use a bloody spirit level on the wires and posts up North', I said to him.

I knew what he was up to, he was deliberately trying to find things wrong so he could cut down on what he had to pay us.

'Well, I suppose it's not bad', he finally said, 'but there's more work I want you to do, I'll pay when it's all done'.

That was it as far as I was concerned.

'Look', I said, 'we're doing you a favour, not the other way around! We're camped here like kangaroos, you haven't supplied a thing. We're leaving and I want the money you owe us now.'

He gave us a little bit more money, it was nowhere near what he owed us, and I had to work hard to get that much out of him. The whole thing left me fed up. It seemed to me that the men who owned land were the same everywhere, be it in Perth or the North.

We went back to Perth for a few more days and then visited some friends in Bullsbrook. After that we headed back to Hedland. I left Susie and the family in Hedland so they could holiday a bit longer, I went out to Mullyie and started doing some odd jobs around the place. While the family was in Hedland my boy Johnny got an offer of a good job on Pippingarra Station, so he decided to take that. It was 1952 by then and he was only seventeen turning eighteen, but he was keen to strike out on his own. I was sad to lose him because we'd always been close, but I knew what it was like to be young and wanting a bit of excitement.

Susie and the kids came out to Mullyie three weeks later and we slipped back into our old routine. Susie loved Mullyie, she loved the life and the land. It was a good place for fish and kangaroos and there was plenty of water there.

We worked there happily for twelve months, then Ben left and Ray Eggerman took over as manager. Ray was only a young bloke, but he wasn't too hard to work for.

173

We got on well at first, but eventually we came to a parting of the ways over my boy Ronnie. You see, I caught the overseer there growling at Ronnie and blaming him for things which weren't his fault. Ronnie was only a kid of fifteen and I knew he wasn't responsible for what had happened, it was someone else's fault. I wasn't going to stand by and see him take the blame, I'd had to do that myself when I was young and I didn't want my kids being stuck with the same thing. I had a row with the overseer and told him to pick on someone his own size.

Then I went to Ray and complained to him about what had happened. He didn't seem to know much about it and wasn't that interested, but my blood was boiling by then so I yelled, 'We're not dogs Ray! I won't have Ronnie being treated like that by the overseer or anyone else. Tell him to pick on the big blokes and leave the kids alone. You just remember that the shearers are only halfway through, if I walked off now you'd be left in the shit with your hands full of work.'

He wasn't pleased with the way I was carrying on so he walked off mumbling.

That made me madder still. I said, 'Right, we'll see the shearing through and then we're off!'

Really, I'd like to have left straight away, but in those days you couldn't allow yourself that luxury. You never knew when you might be wanting a job there again, so it was always best to leave on reasonable terms.

After the shearing was finished and the sheep were back in their paddocks, we left.

I went into Hedland and tried to get a job on the wharf but they were still funny to blackfellas. There was no shortage of labour then because the war was over so they preferred to hire whitemen.

Marie got married, so Susie and I were left with just Ronnie, Doreen, Willie and Josie. Johnny had left Pippingarra and gone north to Derby to work, and although he would come back for visits over the following years, he never stayed. He liked the Kimberleys and later on, the Northern Territory. He was a good son, he always kept in touch and never took advantage of me. He was a very hard worker, if I had've been able to I would have bought him a station.

I managed to find some work on Wallareenya Station, the boss was a good fella, but Susie wasn't happy there. She was pining for Mullyie. I'd been there six months when I received a letter from Ray Eggerman asking me to come back. It wasn't exactly an apology, but it was as good as. He hadn't been able to get anyone to take my place and he was asking me to come back on my own terms. He said I could be my own boss and he wouldn't interfere with my work in any way. I talked it over with the family and of course they were all keen to go back. They had a great affection for Mullyie Station.

We stayed there happily after that. In 1954 I applied to have our children included on our Citizenship Certificate. I was wanting them to have what I saw as their freedom. I went into the Marble Bar Police Station and made a statement saying what my job was, where we lived, how old the children were and when they were born. Later I went to court and the judge asked me how I treated them, whether they went to school and that sort of thing. They were finally granted their freedom towards the end of 1954 and their names were published in the *Government Gazette* in December of that year. Ronnie left us then to strike off on his own, that just left Susie and I with Willie, Doreen and Josie.

I stayed in the Bar for a while after that because there wasn't any station work. We made ends meet by cooking kangaroo, living on the bit of money we'd saved and prospecting. Susie and I loved to go out bush for a poke around.

One time when we were out looking for tin we came across five little boars. I don't know what had happened to their mother because she was nowhere around and the pigs were only babies. I stuffed them all inside my shirt and we took them back into the Bar.

One died, we kept two, who we named Billy and Jimmy, and gave the other two away. They were wonderful pets, they followed us everywhere. The trouble was they were very greedy and the more we fed them the more they wanted. They got very big. This made it difficult if we wanted to shift our camp into the bush or anything like that. We couldn't leave Billy and Jimmy behind, they were part of the family and had to come with us. The trouble was getting them up into the back of the truck. They were used

175

to me lifting them on and off, but they'd grown so fat it was now almost impossible. They didn't help either. I'd start lifting one up and he would go all floppy and start grunting and groaning, that made him feel even heavier. People who saw me trying to lift them used to laugh. They reckoned I'd spoilt them.

We moved out to Warralong Station and I took them with me but I was starting to think that they were more trouble than they were worth. Susie and I had a tent we were sleeping in, and do you think they'd sleep outside? No! They came in and dug a big hole under each of our beds and slept there. You could just see their noses sticking out.

On very hot days they'd lie there all day while I was out fencing. As we came in you'd see these two big, fat pigs running to meet us as if to say, 'Where have you been all day?' They'd be singing out to us grunting and calling, they were so excited to see us. I'd stop the truck and lift them on for a ride back to the camp.

They grew so big that in the end I just found it impossible to handle them. We moved back into the Bar and even though it upset us, we both agreed we just couldn't go on the way we were with those pigs. There were plenty of people wanting them for pork and they thought we were mad not to eat them ourselves, but we just couldn't bring ourselves to do it.

In the end we gave one to a friend and one to the policeman. We knew they were going to be eaten, but we tried not to think about it. But, those two fellas both made the same mistake, they didn't kill them straight away. Their kids all palled up with the pigs and when they came home at night Billy and Jimmy would run out and greet them. After three days they just couldn't bring themselves to kill them.

'You and your bloody pigs, Jack', they said to me, 'they're just like human beings, we can't eat them. They've become family pets!'

I was called back to work on Mullyie again after that. Ray got me to take some sheep over to Shaw River for shearing. I took them over, brought them back and then took the next mob over to get shorn and so on and so on until all the sheep were done.

While I was on Mullyie I began to think about moving down to Perth. It wasn't that I was unhappy or that I didn't like station life, it was just that it wasn't getting me anywhere in the long run. I was tired of not having a wage I could depend on all year round. I was in my fifties by then and wanting something different. All my life I'd wanted to own something of my own. I knew now that I would never be able to own a station because I would never have that much money but I was thinking that it might be possible for me to buy a house. The idea had first come to me when I was granted my Citizenship and the magistrate said that I had to live like a whiteman in a house. The idea of having a house had stuck with me, and I thought if I could buy a real good one in Perth, as well as get work there, it might give us all a better future.

I mentioned my idea of getting a house and job in Perth to the cook on Mullyie, who I knew would be returning to Perth when his contract was over.

'You'd have to be prepared to pay three thousand pounds for a house down there', he told me, 'that won't get you a mansion, but it'd be all right'.

'Three thousand? Well, I haven't got that much but I have got sixty quid I could use as a deposit. Do you think that amount would be acceptable as a deposit?'

'Yes, I think so.'

'When you return to Perth, could you put a deposit down on a house if I gave you the money?'

'All right.'

I suppose it was a silly thing to do but he seemed like an okay bloke and I thought that I could fix the rest up when I went to Perth on my holidays. I was hoping to be able to arrange to pay it off bit by bit.

Anyway, I gave this bloke my sixty quid and he was supposed to get back in touch with me, but he didn't. I waited and waited. In the end I went to the police and they said they'd try and trace him. They contacted me a few weeks later and said they'd found him and that he still had my money and was going to put it down on a house in Midland.

He did this and wrote to me and said when I came to Perth to contact Frank White, as it was his house I was buying.

I came down as soon as I could, booked into the YMCA and caught a taxi out to White's place. His missus couldn't show me the house quick enough. I can't say I was happy with the place, I was disappointed because as far as I was concerned it was only partly built, the ceiling was missing in the main bedroom and there were other things that needed doing.

Frank came along while I was inspecting it and asked me what I thought of the place. I pointed out the ceiling and the other things and he said, 'Oh, don't worry about all that, I'll get it done'. He pointed to a block of land nearby and said, 'You see that land over there?'

'Yes.'

'It'd make a good place for a garage. It just needs fencing and a brick front put up. You could wreck cars in the grounds and then sell the parts in the shop.'

'Oh yes', I said. It sounded like a good idea, I knew there was money to be made in cars.

'I need a partner', Frank said, 'the bloke who paid me the deposit for the house said you were interested in working in Perth. If you put in two hundred quid, I'll get the cyclone fencing done and the brick front put up. It would be a business we could run together and we'll split everything fifty-fifty.'

It sounded all right to me, he seemed to know what he was talking about and he agreed to fix the house up before I moved down permanently and to let me pay it off bit by bit as well. I returned later and gave him the two hundred quid he'd asked for. I had very high hopes then for myself and my family.

Just before I left Perth to go back North I had a run in with a barmaid in a hotel. She refused to serve me. I said to her, 'I've got my Citizenship'.

I showed her my card but she said, 'Look, I don't care what you've got, it doesn't make any difference to me. I'm not serving blacks.' That experience kind of threw cold water on things. It didn't matter how hard you tried, some people just wouldn't give you a go.

I went back to Hedland and told the family what we were doing. They were quite excited about it all, but weren't too sure if they'd be happy away from the North. To tell you the truth, I wasn't too sure myself, but I figured it was worth a try.

We decided that I would go to Perth first and fix up some

furniture for the house and they would all come down later.

When I returned to Perth, Frank had the fencing done and the brick front up but the house was exactly the same. I asked him about it, but he said he hadn't had time and would fix it all up later. I decided to give him the benefit of the doubt.

Frank then told me that the business he had with me was just one of many businesses he had in Perth and that he would be away most of the time working these other places and I would have to run it on my own. I wasn't really happy about this arrangement, but I was willing to give it a go.

I worked long hours stripping down all the cars and separating out the parts. I sold a couple of cars outright to men who were going to fix them themselves and I found an electrician in Perth who wanted to buy all our generators.

Business seemed to be quite good at first and I soon ended up with a few hundred pounds, which I stored away to show Frank when he came back.

When I'd showed him how much we'd made I was expecting him to give me half back because that was our arrangement but instead he only gave me a quarter. I wasn't happy at all, but decided to continue on and see if he changed. He was still finding excuses not to finish off the house.

When the family finally came down the house was still the same, business had dropped off and the little bit that Frank was giving me wasn't enough to meet the payments on the house as well as feed and clothe us. I kept asking Frank to fix the house and tackled him about the money too, but it was like talking to a brick wall. In the end I got so fed up I decided it might be best to go back North.

I went into the head office of the Mark Reuben Pastoral Company. Miss Harding was the secretary there and she knew me.

'Hello Jack', she said, 'what can I do for you?'

'I want to go home', I said, 'my bloody boss is a crook. Are there any station jobs going?'

'Always got a job for you Jack, you're our best worker. When do you want to leave Perth?'

'Soon as possible!'

'Right, I'll book you in for next week.' There was only one flight a week in those days.

After that I went and saw the Midland Shire Council and told them about the trouble between Frank and me. I thought they might be able to give me some advice on how I could get my money off Frank, seeing as how our business was in the Midland area. The bloke I saw was sympathetic.

'If you had have come to us before you went into business we would have told you not to do it. There's been a lot of trouble with that bloke, he'll rob you left, right and centre. The only advice I can give you is to get out while the going's good.'

'What about what I've paid him for the house and business?'

'Do you have anything in writing?'

'Nothing.'

'Then there's nothing you can do because as far as the law goes it's only your word against his. I'm sorry, I really am.'

He wasn't half as sorry as I was! I went and saw Frank and told him I was leaving. He was angry and went on about how he wouldn't let me go.

I said, 'I'm going, whether you like it or not! You've been very unfair with me, your word's worth nothing!'

'I haven't been unfair', he said, 'I've been very fair to let you stay in a house you don't even own, isn't that fair?'

'You call that bloody fair? You've broken every promise you ever made. The house is falling down, I do all the work in the business and get none of the money, you're just a bloody crook!'

I left the following Tuesday. I had to kiss all my money goodbye because I had no proof he'd ever received any. I went back out to Mullyie Station where Ray Eggerman, the manager, put me in charge of a mustering camp and sent me over to Ettrick. Ettrick had once been a separate station but Reuben had combined it with Mullyie and ran both stations as one.

I'd been home two months when I received a letter from Frank asking me to come back. I was that bloody angry I didn't even reply. There was no point in doing anything with that bloke because he wouldn't give you a pinch of shit.

Station work was irregular and I'd never get rich on it, but at least you were paid what you were promised.

180

16
Working On
1961-1971

With the little money I still had I took up some land in the Bar so we would have somewhere more permanent to stay during our breaks from station life. It was a mining lease and cost me fifteen pounds for two acres. I made a camp on it, sunk a well and put a windmill up. During that time I received word that my brother Jimmy Watson had died and been buried in Roebourne. We'd seen each other only now and then over the years, but there had always been a family bond between us. We would always greet each other with, 'Hello brother', and give each other something to show that we recognised what our relationship was.

When I went back to Mullyie I was sent out to Bungalow Station to help with the mustering and shearing. Wally Plant was the manager there at the time and when the work was finished he said, 'I'm finishing up here Jack and going over to manage De Grey. If you and any boys you know want a good job I'll give you one.'

There was no work on at Mullyie at the time so I thought I might as well try De Grey.

When I arrived out there with a couple of other lads who were wanting work, I expected some quarters for us all. The shearers' quarters would have done.

I said to Wally, 'Where do we camp?'

'Down near the river, plenty of food and water down there.'

'Yeah? What about rain?'

'No rain about.'

181

I didn't say anything, I just took the boys and camped down there for a few days to see how things would work out. After three days there wasn't even a hint of any other quarters being provided. I decided to pack it in. I wasn't going to be treated like that anymore.

As we were leaving Wally came running after us saying, 'Jack, the house will be ready soon, you can go from the river into there'.

That was a lot of bulldust because the house had been empty the whole time we were there and no one had been doing any work on it.

'Look Wally', I said, 'if we don't get a house now, we're going. I don't have to put up with this kind of treatment, it's not the early days anymore you know!'

'I don't want to lose you and the boys Jack, come and I'll show you your quarters.'

He took us over to the house, it was filthy, dusty and bare. No beds, no table, no chairs, no nothing!

'You got a table to put in here?' I asked.

'I don't think so.'

'Well, I seen one down in the shed.'

We walked down to have a look. Wally examined that table over and over, he kept finding excuses not to give it to us. I held my ground, it was a rickety old thing anyway, but it was the principle of it all. Wally was being just plain mean.

In the end he said, 'All right, take it!'

I worked on De Grey for a few months making water tanks and doing general maintenance work, but I found Wally really hard to work for. I knew much more about station work than him, yet he kept finding fault with everything I did. Some of his suggestions were bloody silly and I knew if I did things his way the job would be no good. He'd tell me how to fix a tank or a fence and I'd say, 'Look Wally, if you do it that way, it won't last. It's better to do it this way because it will save you money in the long run.'

He didn't like me talking like that, he liked to play Big Boss all the time. In the end I decided to pack it in. He was just too prickly.

It was too hot then to even think about getting work at Mullyie so I went back into the Bar and managed to pick up a job with the public works. I was heading towards sixty by then and it turned out the job I got lumbered with was harder than the station. I had to sit in the sun all day cutting up railway lines with a hacksaw and they don't call Marble Bar the hottest town in Australia for nothing.

I'd been there a few months when Wally came into town one day trying to round up men to help him mustering.

When he asked me I said, 'I'll only do stockwork'. I wasn't going to have him correcting me about every little thing again. At least if I was doing stockwork I'd be able to get away from him.

He agreed to that and then I said, 'And when the stockwork's finished, the shearing's finished, I'm finished, we're finished'.

What I didn't know at the time was that Ray Eggerman was wanting men too, Wally had just beaten him to us. When the work was finished on De Grey, Wally took us all over to Mullyie.

When we arrived there Ray sang out, 'You ready to start Jack?'

'I haven't got off the bloody truck yet!'

'Well you better hurry up before Wally changes his mind and takes you back!'

'I'm not going back', I laughed.

We mustered for Mullyie and then stayed on for a few months seeing the shearing through and doing odd jobs around the place, including some fencing.

When the work cut out I was back in the Bar. I got a job with a bloke who had a tin mine on the Brockman River.

It was my job to work the cone, which is like a big dish that catches the tin and draws it down into a bucket.

The work was all right, but the boss was no good. He had me going day and night and wasn't coming forth with any pay either. We'd agreed that I was to be paid once a fortnight, but in four weeks I hadn't seen a penny. I asked him about it of course but he just kept saying, 'You'll get your money!'

That was all very well, but what was the family supposed to live on in the meantime? I had to book everything up. It was getting towards Christmas when I decided to chuck it in.

Just before I left the boss came to me and said, 'I'm off for holidays Jack, I'll send your pay up, should be here by Friday'.

I'd been there five months by then! I was stupid, I should have left as soon as he failed to pay me the first time. The thing was,

183

I had no other job to go to and I hung in there hoping the money would come through. He sent me the money eventually, but not all of it. There was no holiday pay and he'd taken a bit out for some food I'd eaten!

The manager at Warrawagine must have heard I needed a job because he offered me one as cook. Our kids had all left by then, and even though the younger ones popped back and forth, we were mainly on our own. Susie and I took the job. She did the cakes and fancy stuff and I did the bread and meat. It was a good job and we were happy there.

However, after three months the managers changed and the new boss reckoned we were being paid far too much and that the station couldn't afford it. He also thought we didn't work hard enough and wanted us to do extra jobs besides cooking. We saw the job through and then I was called over to Mullyie to fix some windmills.

When that finished Warrawagine contacted me again to do some fencing. I had no other work at the time so I couldn't knock it back. I wasn't there long when my offsider decided to pull out.

'I can't work with that boss', he said. 'You can stay, Jack, but I've had enough, I'm off.'

I knew what he meant, I thought I might leave myself then but the boss came to me and said, 'I'll show you another job Jack, you might like to do it'.

It was a mile of fencing that needed doing over near Yarrie Station.

'Give you fifteen quid for the mile', he said after he'd showed it to me.

'No, worth more than that, it's hard country. I won't do it under fifty quid for the mile.'

We went back to the homestead to talk it over. He couldn't understand why I wouldn't do it for fifteen quid. I tried to explain.

'Hard country, hard work. I've got to drive my own truck, use my own materials and pay someone to help me. For fifteen quid it's just not worth it.'

'Can't pay anymore than that.'

'Well, if you can't pay anymore, I can't do anymore.' I left the next morning.

I was called over to De Grey then, Wally Plant had dropped

dead coming out of the toilet and they'd put Ray Eggerman in charge. He took Susie on as cook and I went back to the usual station work. I put in four miles of fencing, sunk a well, fixed some windmills and made a couple of tanks.

It was 1963 by then and the rivers were running very high that year because there'd been a lot of rain.

While I was on De Grey I received word that my old brother Jack Doherty had died. He had been living on and off between Marble Bar and his daughter's place out near the Comet mine. We had always seen each other whenever we could and had a few beers together.

Jack had been given an invalid pension because of his eyes in the end so he hadn't had to worry about money the way I had.

I was very upset about him going, I wanted to get in to his funeral but the rivers were uncrossable. Later, when the water was down, I went and saw his grave and paid my last respects. We had shared a lot of personal things with one another over the years. Just thinking about him now brings tears to my eyes.

That was the same year that I decided to give up the grog completely. I was a pretty heavy drinker by then. I seemed to cut down, then build up, cut down, then build up. There'd been times when I'd tried to give it up but I hadn't been strong enough to hold out against my mates. They'd say things like, 'If you won't drink with us, you're not one of us', and call me a woman and things like that. They'd make you feel so bad you'd give in to them and get rotten drunk.

Anyway, what happened was this. I had been sinking a well with some other blokes. We knocked off at midday on Saturday and went into Dalgety's to buy some grog and relax a bit. I backed the jeep up to the store and said, 'A case of beer and a gallon of plonk'. They loaded it on, then we did a bit of shopping and had a few beers before we headed for home. On the way home we drank a few more bottles and a few more and so on. Around midnight we had a feed and then we all went to bed.

The following morning I was as sick as a dog. I was going to the toilet every few minutes and that wasn't helping at all. I was in terrible pain. I thought my end had come. I was sick all day Sunday and no better Monday morning, so the boys had to go to work without me. I never started to come good until late that afternoon and then I decided, no more grog.

When the boys came out to check on me I said, 'You fellas can have all that grog, I'm finished! I'm never touching it again. If you don't want it then I'll throw it down the creek.' They wanted it all right!

Since then I've had many people try to get me to take a drink. They get angry when you won't drink with them. I just ignore them. If they get really stuck into me I say, 'You fellas can talk all you want, I won't change my mind. You want to get drunk good. Here's a quid, go and make yourselves sick.'

People say I have a very strong will, and I think that's true. I haven't had a drink since that day.

Work cut out on De Grey after that, Eggerman suggested I cut and stack some posts to fill in time till some more work came along. However, Marie and her bloke came out and saw me and told me about a job they thought I should go for.

'What are you doing?' they asked when they saw me.

'I'm sitting on the verge of nothin'!' I told them.

'Kathleen Investments are looking for a man who knows the Moolyella area.'

'Is it a good job?'

'You'll be a boss.'

'How about the pay?'

'Seems all right.'

'Well, there's nothing doing here, I might give it a go.'

I applied for the job and got it. I was the Pit Supervisor. It was a job where you used your mind more than your muscles. I was in charge of fifteen men, some on dozers and some on scrapers. I had to direct them where to dig. We were sampling the value of the ground for tin. We'd cut a hole anywhere between ten and twenty feet deep and take a sample. If it was good, we'd strip the place, if it was no good I'd move the dozers on. I was very happy working there.

While I was with Kathleen Investments they had a referendum. Everyone in Australia had to vote on whether Aborigines should be allowed to be Australians without having to apply for their Citizenship. You can guess what I voted. We were free then, you could wipe your goona* on your Citizenship paper after that. Of course, some of us had felt like doing that when we first got it. That referendum was very important because before that we weren't Australians by law and now we were.

I continued on with Kathleen Investments for five years and during that time there were twelve different managers. Fortunately, that didn't affect my job because they were all very good men. You see, if the company felt production was falling, they put a new bloke in charge, it was silly really because they were all good at their job.

All the managers were wonderful, bar one. He had worked overseas and I think he thought he could treat me the way he treated the Malays. He liked to interfere and tell you what to do. No one had ever complained about the work I did before, I knew that Moolyella area better than anyone alive. I got fed up in the end and quit, he was just too difficult to work for.

Susie and I went prospecting for six months after that and then I landed another job with the Shaw River Alluvial Company doing exploration work. I was my own boss and very happy about it too. I was paid one hundred dollars a week and all my fuel and car expenses. I really enjoyed that job because I didn't have to account for my time. Also, they trusted me to do the right thing by them.

Their head office was in New South Wales and they sent money over to take up whatever leases I thought were good. I always returned any leftover money. They gave up on the exploration in the end because it became uneconomical for them to be based in Sydney and have leases in Western Australia. The job only lasted six months, but it was one of the best jobs I ever had.

I took on a few odd jobs after that and in between I would go prospecting to bring in a few extra dollars.

In 1969 Susie and I were made legal guardians for seven of our grandchildren aged between six and fourteen years old. Their mother was sick and we didn't want to see them go into a home. They stayed with us until slowly, as they grew up, they left one by one to make their own way in the world.

*   Goona: faeces.

17

A Government Man
1971 onwards

I was granted the old age pension in 1971 and Susie was granted it the next year. From then on if anyone asked me who I was working for I'd say, 'I'm a government man now, Gough Whitlam's my boss'.

Gough Whitlam had come to power as Prime Minister in 1972 and he did a lot for Aboriginal people. I didn't mind him being my boss.

While I had been off the booze for years by then Susie hadn't cut down at all, in fact, she was drinking more than ever. The kids and grandchildren all tried to get her to cut down. She knew that it wasn't good for her, but she just didn't seem to have the willpower to be able to say no to her mates. They were going downhill themselves and wanted to take others with them.

Even though the grog was getting the better of her, she was still cooking and cleaning and making sure the kids were all right. She'd still go out bush now and then with the grandchildren and shoot a roo. That was Susie, she was a tough, high-spirited woman. She'd had a hard life, like a lot of women did in those days, but she'd struggled through.

Of course our marriage had its ups and downs. Sometimes there were more downs than ups, and we'd nearly divorced a couple of times. Sometimes I would go away on a job on my own and that would help. We started to live fairly separate lives, even though we remained married.

I think one of the main problems was the grog, or maybe that just added to everything else, I don't know.

I cannot say too strongly how I feel about the alcohol problem amongst my people today. I've been through it, I've seen the effects in my own family, I cannot say how important it is to stay off the booze. I know some people will be thinking, well he used to drink himself. I'm not saying I'm a saint. I set a bad example myself for a while, but I'm setting a good one now. I'm being strong and not giving in to those who want you to drink just for the sake of it. I used to go along with my mates for fear of losing them, now I figure if that's so important to them then they weren't proper mates in the first place. I've lost friends through refusing to drink.

I reckon grog is killing over half our people today and making the rest bloody silly. I don't think we were meant to have grog in our bodies. The Mulba is not like the European who's been drinking it for generations. Booze has only been in this country two hundred years, it just makes me wonder if there isn't something in the Mulba's body that can't cope with it.

Anyway, I can truthfully say that it was booze that killed Susie, nothing else. In 1977 she was in and out of Port Hedland Hospital. I remember picking her up once and taking her back to the Bar. She seemed a lot better and I hoped she would stay off it for a while. I fixed the kids up in the morning and then I made her a cup of tea.

'Here's your tea Mum', I said, but she didn't want it.

She got up and went and sat outside under our old bower shed.

I could see she was a bit funny, different to the other times she'd been sick. I wasn't quite sure what to do. I tidied up the house and then went and checked on her again.

She didn't look right to me so I said, 'I think I better take you to see Matron, Mum'.

'All right, I'll come with you.'

I took her up to the hospital and Matron said, 'I think she's pretty crook Jack. The doctor will be here at eleven, I think we better get her back to Hedland Hospital as soon as possible.'

The doctor came and by the time they put her on the plane to Hedland she was unconscious. It was Christmas Eve.

I packed up the kids and went into Hedland myself. I went and saw Susie in hospital and she seemed to be all right, she was sitting up talking.

I hung around until the end of December because they wouldn't let her out. I returned to the Bar the beginning of January and had only been home a few days when Matron called me up.

'I've just got word she's very low Jack. Where will you be if there's any news?'

'You can find me at the postmaster's house, his wife is helping out with the kids.'

Four o'clock that afternoon I was sitting by the door when I saw this white uniform come in. It was Matron, she leant down and put her arms around me and said, 'Susie's gone'.

I flew her body back to the Bar to be buried, because I felt that was where she belonged. I couldn't complain about our marriage anymore then. She'd gone and left me behind after forty-two years. We'd lived through thick and thin, good times and bad. We'd had a rough life and been forced to eat tucker we didn't like, but we'd raised six kids and survived. I felt that was something.

When the funeral was over, me and the grandkids I was still guardian to went back to my block and had a camp.

I was lying on my bed with my arm over my head when my cattle dog gave one sharp yelp. The kids were all asleep and I didn't look up at first because I thought it was probably my son Johnny coming in, as I was expecting him. When I did look up who did I see sitting on the end of my bed but Susie. I was so stunned I rolled back and hid my face, when I looked again she was still there. She sat there for a while and then just disappeared.

The next day I went and saw some of our people and told them what had happened. They said, 'Yes, that's right, we seen her too'.

Later some of the children and grandchildren saw her. She continued to appear to different ones on and off in Port Hedland and Marble Bar for twelve months, and then she was gone. I think it takes them that long to say goodbye to their family.

The last contact I had with her was when I was camped at Mort Lockyer's house keeping an eye on his missus while he was in hospital. I was lying on the lawn on my back when a pebble suddenly hit me on the chest. In the morning I picked it up and looked at it. It was a shingle from the river. I thought that was strange because even though we were near the river it wouldn't have rolled uphill and bounced on me. I told Manny Lockyer about it and he said, 'Ah Jack, that's your last call, you won't hear from her again now'. He was right, I didn't.

You see, there's a lot of things to do with the spiritual world that we don't understand, but that doesn't mean it's not true. Mulbas know a lot about the spirit. Someone you're related to might have died, they could be miles away, but the jibari will tell you. You might just have a feeling and know it's true, or you might be sitting inside your house and see a light go on in the dark outside and then suddenly go out again. You might be sitting outside in daytime and see them appear to you. That's jibari, it's the signal or message that says they've just gone.

Seeing people after they've died, seeing their spirit, is a common thing with Mulbas. I had heard about it happening to different ones all my life but had never actually experienced it myself until Susie went. That's not to say that I hadn't had a similar thing when Jack Doherty died. There were times when I would feel him very close to me, as if to say, 'Don't worry brother, I'm still going strong'.

In 1980 Clancy McKenna died. I'd only seen him the day before and we'd had a wonderful talk about the old days.

We often talked about the book he'd written, he was very proud of it. He reckoned he'd got stuck into all the squatters, the only one he'd praised up was Tommy Mallett. I felt proud of him too, it was a big thing to have a book written about you when you couldn't read or write. I was thinking I might like to do that one day.

I was very shocked when Clancy died. I had a feeling he was - sick, but his death shocked me. I really miss him.

I lost my son Johnny that year too, that was a real shock to me because I'd only seen him six months before and he'd looked so well. I think he must have known then he had cancer, but didn't tell us.

I had his body flown back from Alice Springs because I didn't want him being buried in strange country.

After he died I sometimes felt him close to me. I didn't see him the way I saw Susie, but he was there just the same, as if to say, 'Don't worry about me Dad, I'm still with you'. I was terribly cut up about losing him.

I eventually sold my land in the Bar, there were too many memories there. I moved into Port Hedland and went from place to place staying with different ones. I didn't seem to be able to settle anywhere.

I'm happier now because I have my own little pensioner unit in Port Hedland and it's very nice. I have meals on wheels and play bingo and a nice white lady comes in once a week and cleans up for me. I've got a bad knee so I can't get around as much as I'd like and I had to let my driver's licence go a few years back because of my eyes.

For the past three years or so I've been coming to Perth and staying with Sally and Paul and working on this book. Just when I think it's finished she finds another question to ask me and I find myself going on and on like a broken old record. I make her promise that'll be the end of it and she just says, 'We'll see', and then before I know it she's dragged out something else!

I suppose we're pretty evenly matched when it comes to willpower.

Everyone keeps saying to me, 'When's your book coming out Jack?' And for three years I've been telling them, 'Soon, she's nearly finished it!' I wonder if they really believe I'm doing one.

I've been wanting to finish it quickly so I can show it off but she goes on about doing it properly, and in the end I've had to come round to her way of thinking, because she's used my arguments against me. She says, 'Jack, you're the one who goes on about how if station work isn't done properly it won't stand the test of time, well, it's the same with writing a book'. What can I say? It's 1989 now, I'm still talking and she's still writing.

She told me the other day we're getting towards the end and that people will like it, so I'm pleased about that. Then she asked me to think about what I'd like to say in the final chapter.

'I thought we'd done the final chapter.'

'Well, yes, we have Jack, but I thought we could add another one and you could talk about how you feel about your life now and perhaps you might want to say something about the future for young Aboriginal people.'

You see what I mean, she always finds something extra to put in.

192

Jack McPhee, Marble Bar, 1985. (Photograph by Denis O'Meara)

EPILOGUE
Number One

I've had a think, and before I say anything, I want to say this. The way I see things is based on the way I've had to live, please remember that.

I want to talk about stations. They were built on black labour. On sour bread, damper, roo meat and whippings. The squatter had it hard too, because life in those days was hard, but they made money out of it. Two generations on their families are all right, ours aren't. Many of them are now wealthy men with land and businesses and respect, we have nothing.

I can only explain it like this. Two friends of mine were working on a station. The manager, who was an okay fella, went away and put a new bloke in charge. There was a good garden there, my friend looked after it while his wife worked in the house. Now the new boss loved watermelon and my friend had some in the garden. He was told he wasn't allowed to have any of those melons, even though my friend had grown them himself. Instead, when the boss had eaten the good part, he would throw him the leftovers. For years the whiteman's been getting the sweet part of the melon and the blackman, if he's lucky, has had to be content with leftovers.

I can honestly say that I have tried very hard in my life to live quietly and to better myself and my family. When I was just a native I was told that if I wanted to get on in the world I had to become a whiteman, but when I tried to do that people would look at me and say, 'Oh you're just a native!'

Some people think all Aborigines are the same, yet we have

different tribal groups, different languages, different customs. Our colour isn't even the same, some of us are black, some are brown, some are only light. Some of us can speak language and some know only English; some can read and write and some can't. Some of us are no-hopers and alcoholics, and others are working men who know right from wrong. People see a few rotten apples and write us off. I've known whitemen who were bastards and I've known whitemen who were the best mates a man could have. I'm sick of people thinking we all look and think the same. A man should be judged on his own and not as part of a group.

Now, about Mulba things. I think it's very sad that some of our people feel ashamed of the old culture, especially our languages and dancing. I can speak five Aboriginal languages and I can sing in seven. I know many Mulbas who can speak their language but won't. Sometimes when I'm sitting in the South Hedland shopping centre, I wait until I see some of my countrymen coming and then I call out to them in language. They get very embarrassed. I tell them I'm not ashamed of my language and they shouldn't be either. I'll speak my language anywhere.

You see, their idea is this. They think if they talk language the white people might think they're running them down. Over the years I've seen the same thing happen at corroboree time. White people are very interested in corroborees, but my people get worried about singing in language in case someone says, 'Oh speak bloody English will ya?!'

For many years there was ill feeling in the North between black and white. No one wanted us to go up in the world, we were classed next to a dog. I'm happy to say that's changing. However, I don't agree with some of the black people who won't speak to white people. They're getting silly themselves now. They blame the white people for everything, especially the past, but I think there are some things happening now that they're responsible for. Young people drinking and stealing, old people gambling everything, mothers and fathers not wanting to work or look after their kids. We had none of that in my day.

It's hard because Mulbas see things differently. We'd rather lend twenty dollars to someone than pay the rent. If people owe us money and won't pay we just walk away. We've got to be in a group

195

all the time, we won't spread out and make an independent living for ourselves. The grandmothers won't say no to anything. They keep taking in all the children the young people don't want instead of making them care for those kids themselves.

Also, if things are all right now like people say, then why are all these boys dying in gaol? I just can't understand that and it really worries me. I am very worried about the young Aboriginal boys and girls and what's going to become of them if they keep on the way they are. I know there are some good ones who try their best, that's why I'm going to make a scholarship, to help the ones that are trying to help themselves. I want to do that, and I want to be remembered as someone who made mistakes like everyone else, but who came through in the end and did something good for his people.

I'm roughly eighty-four now and I've been through a lot in my life. I have to tell you that it's only as you get to the end of your life that you start to realise what things are really important to you. I've been through the Exemption Certificate and Citizenship and I've struggled to live up to the whiteman's standard, but here I am, old, and good for nothing, and what keeps coming back to me? Dances, singing, stories the old people used to tell. Every night I lie in bed and sing myself to sleep with all my old corroboree songs. I go over and over them and I remember that part of my life. They're the things I love, they're the things I miss.

My friend Peter Coppin, I think of him as a young bloke, but he must be in his sixties by now, you should hear him talk about me. He points to me in front of real young fellas and says, 'You see that fella there, he looks like a whiteman now, but I remember him all dressed up in cockatoo feathers, paint and pearlshell, singing and dancing, doing all the things blackfellas do. He's the only old one left who remembers how it used to be, he's the only one who's number one fella to me.'